D0756188

yan and the christmas tree

Jun Machida

This edition published in the UK by
acorn book company
PO Box 191
Tadworth
Surrey KT20 5YQ

email: info@acornbook.co.uk

www.acornbook.co.uk

ISBN 0-9534205-8-2

British Library Cataloguing in Publication Data.
A catalogue record for this book is available from the British Library.

Translated from the Japanese by Noriko Kajihara and Chris Mulhern
First published in Japan by Publisher Michitani Co. Ltd, Tokyo
Copyright ©Jun Machida, 1997
This translation copyright © acorn book company, 2004
Printed and bound in Great Britain by The Cromwell Press, Ltd.

THE
ARTS
COUNCIL
OF ENGLAND

We would like to thank the Arts Council
of England for their assistance
in the publication of this title.

yan and the christmas tree

Yan in the café

The warm tide from the Marmara Sea met the cold from the Black Sea and Istanbul was covered in fog. It was New Year's Day. I had stayed the night in an old hostelry not far from the waterfront. It was an ancient place but smelt somehow familiar. I went down the steep slope of Beyol. The pier jutting out into Golden Horn Bay was shrouded in mist.

The passenger ferry loomed up out of the whiteness and we went zigzagging up the bay stopping here and there to pick up or set down passengers. The boat was moored neatly against the pier. I went down the gangplank with the old man who had been sitting next to me. He was blind in one eye and had probably come here for the same reason as myself, to visit the Mosque of Eyup.* We passed a row of three-story wooden houses with tumbledown balconies, and at the end of the street I caught my first glimpse of the Mosque. It had a solemn, yet vibrant presence.

*Eyup was one of Mohammed's disciples. The Mosque houses his tomb.

I am not a believer myself, so after a while I bowed and went out of the mosque. I was wondering whether the sense of calm it exudes was because it was a sacred place. I saw the old man on the way back chatting in the street, he had a gentle smile on his face.

I had nothing to do for the rest of the day, so instead of taking the ferry I began walking slowly towards the old part of the city down by the sea. I just fancied a stroll and was in no particular hurry. The fog was lifting a little, but the coast on the other side of the bay was still obscured by it, and I was only able to make out the faint outline of the houses a hundred yards ahead.

The way I had come was soon swallowed up in the fog, too. Here and there, the minarets of the mosques were sticking out through the fog, and from these I was able to get a general sense of direction. I wandered along aimlessly. I had a vague idea I was somewhere around the Greek quarter when I noticed a white cat with brown stripes on its back following me. I stroked his head and told him that I was sorry but I had nothing on me to give him. I walked for a long time after that, and came to the Greek Orthodox Cathedral, and there again, I noticed the cat was following about ten yards behind me. When I stopped, he pretended to ignore me and started sniffing the front door of one of the houses.

Near the magnificent Suleymaniye Mosque I went into a little café on the corner of the street. Several old people were enjoying the first day of the New Year in their own way, reading newspapers and chatting. I was sitting there sipping a cup of strong Turkish coffee, when a big cat with a red Turkish hat on sat down beside me, and suddenly started talking. He wanted to know if the cat was mine, he nodded past me and as I looked round, the stripey white cat was sitting on the floor, with its tail coiled, looking thoughtful and serious. I said it wasn't mine, just a stray that had been following me for a while.

To be honest, I was rather taken aback. For a start, the cat in front of me was too big for a cat, and what was more, it was behaving as if it were human, and giving the impression that that was perfectly normal. I was trying to act as if nothing was the matter when I heard my usually cynical inner voice saying: 'Don't panic, there is no need to panic'. As I looked closer, I noticed that the big cat in front of me had similar markings to the one on the floor.

'Really?' the cat said again, 'it must be fond of you. Are you from abroad? From Russia by any chance?'

When I answered, 'from abroad yes, but not from Russia,' he looked slightly disappointed. But then, he changed the topic straight away, and asked, 'Do you like cats?'

'Yes,' I said.

'So do you understand what this cat is trying to tell you?'

'Well, I suppose it's hungry.'

The cat in front of me, shook its head.

'Not at all. Only people who don't know any better would say 'oh, it must want some food,' but look at its eyes carefully. A cat's eyes show their thoughts and dreams, as they change from moment to moment. The eyes tell you what a cat is trying to say. You could write a poem just looking at them for a few seconds. If you look at them for half an hour, you could write a short story, and if you sat and looked into them for a whole day – you'd end up with a magnificent long novel.'

The cat sat back and twitched his whiskers proudly. He had ginger and white stripes on his back, and a white stomach. And the Turkish hat looked quite natural on him, although you don't see that many cats wandering around with Turkish hats on.

The Empire* was in its twilight and was beginning to decline.

* The Ottoman Empire

Yan in the café (getting dark)

I was beginning to get used to the absurd goings on around me, and asked, 'So what do you read in this cat's eyes?'
The cat in front of me looked slightly weary, and told me a few clichéd anecdotes most of which were just versions of gossip I'd already heard. I was reassured by the fact that this cat didn't have much in the way of imagination, in fact there was nothing more remarkable about it other than the very fact of its existence. I more or less told him as much while stroking the head of the other cat which by then had come to sit beneath my chair. The big cat in the Turkish hat didn't seem to be offended and just went on staring off into the distance with his amber eyes.

'You look good in that Turkish hat but the times are changing,' I said changing the topic myself.

'True,' said the cat.

'Revolutions are taking place everywhere aren't they?' I said. 'This country may disappear altogether just like the Russian Empire.'

'It might,' said the cat again. 'It might even end up being governed by a nation that has yet to come into being.'

'Well, despite all the upheaval, some good might come of that,' I said. But that seemed to make the cat almost angry.

'You talk about nations and empires as if they were real, but these are just lines you humans draw on a map. What difference do you think that makes to us cats and other animals? You humans always look down on us anyway.'

'So are you expecting the next revolution to be led by the animals?'

The cat in front of me suddenly burst out laughing, 'Mya, mya, mya, mya. There is no way you can understand our thoughts. Because you can't even read that cat's eyes,' said the cat. 'What a cat wants, its hopes and dreams, are things that humans cannot understand. Although I must admit, I have a feeling that one day I might come across a human who can understand that. Some day perhaps … That's why I go round chatting to people in the hope that one of them might be able to understand. Well, I'm sorry to have taken up so much of your time,' the cat looked as if he was about to get up and leave.

'No, wait a minute, please. I think I can read a story like the one you told me just now. Or, is there a deeper story hidden behind it?'

'That is something your poor imagination cannot handle.'

'Perhaps, but what is it?'

The cat with a Turkish hat opened his mouth after a moment's hesitation.
'It is the story of a fir tree. The eternal fir tree.'

'FIR TREE? … You mean, a fir tree as in F-I-R?'

'Yes.'

'Where did that come from?'

'There is a poem that goes:

'the Future is not enough
Old things and New things are not enough
In the middle of a meadow, all eternity
becomes a sacred fir tree …'

'You mean the Christmas tree you decorate in the corner of your room, is that it?
But why would a cat … ?'

'No, no, no, not at all. You see you don't understand. You don't understand how the whole of eternity can become a solitary fir tree in the middle of a meadow…'

He excused himself, readjusted the Turkish hat, and went out of the café holding the other cat carefully in his paws.

That was the first time I'd seen one cat holding another. As his back disappeared into the fog, he flicked his tail as if to say, 'See you again sometime.'

Perhaps he was going off to read a little bit more in the eyes of the cat he was holding.

I was left pondering what had just happened. It was already dark outside and in the distance I could hear the call for evening prayers.

I ordered another cup of coffee to clear my head, then opened the first page of one of the several books I had bought at random from a bookshop in Eyup, and began reading:

'Strange thing about this town, how you can approach the truth by lying and being lied to…'

CONTENTS

Section 1
Prologue - a Man's Reminiscence from 1921   21

Section 2
The Christmas in the Meadow in 1900 – 1902   37

I   The First Journey, or the Autumn Journey   38
     A Ticket for a Sentimental Journey   38
     Savinski   44

II   The Second Journey, or the Winter Journey   55
     The Iceboat   55
     The Decoration of the Galaxy   64
     The Short Story Writer   80

III The Third Journey, or the Journey in Blizzard 90

IV   The Constellations in the Drawer   95

V   The Fourth Journey,
     or the Late-Summer Journey   102
     The Frozen Moment   102
     The Other Christmas   109

VI The Fifth Journey,
    or the Journey at the Beginning of Winter   117
    The Miracle   117
    The Dance of Snow   121
    The Sculpture of the Rook   125
    The Writer and the Crane   136

VII The Pike   143
     The Arrival of Spring   143
     The First Autumn Breeze   153

VIII The Final Journey,
      or the Autumn Journey Again   165

Section 3
Epilogue - a Man's Reminiscence from 1934   171

A Letter from Chekhov   205
Extracts from an Interview with the Director   207

To Yan

The future is not enough
Old things and New things are not enough
In the middle of a meadow, all eternity
becomes a sacred fir tree …

From 'Winter Celebration' by Boris Pasternak

Section 1 - Prologue, a man's reminiscence from 1921

The faint wail of a train echoed from below the horizon somewhere out of sight beyond the slow-drifting snowclouds. The snow which had been falling in white lace-like patterns had stopped for a while. There was no wind. The darkening sky was covered with thick clouds, creating a fleeting twilight in which it was impossible to tell whether day or night was beginining. The noise of the train echoed from the low-lying cloud.

I had been wandering the snowfield for the last few hours, and the footprints I had left behind went round in a big circle and disappeared. Neither the moon nor the stars were shining and the new snowflakes were being scattered in vain onto the vast, white snowfield. The heavy fur coat I was wearing still smelled of the animals the pelts had come from. I was cursing myself for coming here.There was an orange light in the far distance where the snow clouds and the earth met and I began walking towards it.

After about an hour's walk I came to an inn that looked just like the other farmhouses in these parts. With the last of my strength I knocked at the door. It was opened a little, and a warm light shone through the gap, slanting diagonally across the snowfield. My eyes were blinded by the light and I couldn't even see the silhouette of the person who had opened it.

'Oh, dear. You must be exhausted. Quick, come inside. It's nice and warm in here. Come on in.'

As the light shone on him, I could see from his hat that he was an Orthodox Jew.

'What? A guest at this time of night?' said another man turning over a playing card without looking up. 'Not my day,' he said. He gathered the cards together and went out of the room.

'He's not particularly sociable, I'm afraid. He's uneducated, you see. He can't even write properly at his age. He can add up ok, but he can't do subtraction. But there is no one who knows the forests, the rivers, and the wastelands better than he. By the way, what would you like to eat? I can offer you some shchi* . Oh, no, hang on, yes there's some clay fish* * soup left. He caught them in the marshes the day before yesterday. They're delicious. Hang on, oh, or do you, er, …'

* shchi:A cabbage soup. This time of year it would be made from pickled cabbage.
* * clay fish live in freshwater. Though how he caught them this time of year is anybody's guess.

I was terribly tired and as soon as my body began to warm up I started to feel very sleepy. I was too tired to take in what he was saying and was just nodding without really listening.

I finished the soup which smelt of mud, and the hard bread, and to get away from his talk, I went to lie down on a bench in the corner of the dingy room.

A deep calm sleep came over me... feeling the way forward into the dark forest, the vast empty snowfield, a shallow restless sleep, the morning light on my eyelids... The morning light turned the misty window into a stained glass panel of pale red and deep blue, with the window frame dividing it like a cross.

'Oh, you're awake? You slept well last night. You were so fast asleep I didn't want to wake you up to take you to the guest room at the back. But do please have a look at it before you go. It's one of the best rooms around here. There's even a rug on the floor. That was quite expensive actually. I splashed out almost a year's worth of savings on that because someone told me it was an investment for life. You might think it's just a bit of rug, but it's a treasure for life for my poor self. Longer than that in fact, it'll last till my grandchildren's time. No one else in this village has a rug like it. Apparently, it came all the way from somewhere called, Astrakahn. I don't believe half the story myself. But that was what the merchant said anyway. People all say it is a genuine Persian carpet though. Why not have a look before you go? It won't take a minute. But do have some breakfast first.'

His talk was coming in to my right ear and going out of the left while I spooned in the cold soup. It was tasting more and more disgusting. I interrupted him to ask a question.

'Is there a fir tree standing on its own in the middle of a field anywhere round here?'

'I beg your pardon? A fir tree? We've got so many fir trees around here we have to throw them away. How big do you want it? There are five or six of them round the back already cut. We could make you a very special price. Are you thinking of building a hut or something?'

'No. Have you seen a fir tree with a star at the top of it? A fir tree that's still growing.'

'Don't try and make fun of me just because you've had some fancy education. Men become wiser as they get older, you know. And I'm at least as old as you are. No, in fact I'm much older. So don't think you can make a fool of me just because I'm a simple old man.'

'I am not making a fool of you at all. I'm perfectly serious. Is there a fir tree somewhere around here with a silver star on the top of it?'

'Have you seen it before?'

'No, not exactly…' I didn't know how to explain this, and all I could think of saying was,

'I heard about it from someone else, but I'm sure it's a true story.'

He looked as if he'd finally understood and said triumphantly,

'How nice! Well, that's good. Being able to dream is one of the pleasures of youth. You had a good dream. About a Christmas tree. Hang on, speaking of which, is it Christmas Day today? You must be an Orthodox Christian. Merry Christmas. This is the day you celebrate the birth of your Messiah is it not? Congratulations.'

'Thank you. By the way, do you know the fir tree I'm talking about?'

'You *are* a persistent fellow. No, I don't know.'

He got to his feet impatiently.

He gave me a cup of tea which was so weak it was almost water and then asked for an extortionate price for the night's stay. I just wanted to get out of there as soon as possible, so without even bothering to haggle, I paid up and was about to go.

He suddenly became all friendly again, and said,

'Please do have a look at the rug before you go, it won't take a minute. You only need to take a quick peep at it. Oh, by the way, I'll ask my brother about the fir tree. He knows all about that kind of thing. He may even know about this tree of yours. What do you say?'

I was tempted by that, so I agreed to go and have a look at the rug which was probably nothing special at all.

It was every bit as bad as I'd expected. It was a single-knot weave* and had nothing to commend it. You could say it was 'old', certainly, but you could also say it was just well-worn, and stained with paraffin and paint.

'This isn't from Persia,' I said. 'It's from Kavkaz. It's a very rare specimen. A real rarity. And it's in good condition, for it's age.'

'Is it really? Rare you say? And this pattern is from the Kavkaz region,' repeating what I had just said, and looking very pleased with himself.

Of course, it wasn't from Kavkaz at all. It looked more like something which had been flung out of a commoner's household during the revolution. But anyway. I just wanted to get out of there as soon as I could.

At that point his brother appeared in the doorway.

'Hey! Have you seen a tree with a star on the top of it? This fellow here is looking for it. What do you reckon? Do you know anything about it?'

The brother stared silently into my face, looking just as sullen as before.

*Takes less time to make than a double-knot weave, but is of inferior quality

'Ok, so you don't know. Fine,' said the proprietor. 'I'm sorry, but your friend must have got it wrong. I'm sorry that I can't help you. Happy Christmas, then. Take care,' he said with a business-like expression, and went inside the house shutting the door.

The brother was still standing at the doorway.

As I walked away, he followed me.

'It doesn't exist any more,' he said.

But, I could tell he wanted to say more.

'So, you *do* know about the fir tree with the star on it.'

'No, I don't.'

'Then why do you say 'any more'?'

'I heard about it from a hunter in the next village.'

'What did the hunter say?'

He turned away and started walking quickly.

I threw my bag over my shoulder and hurried to keep up. Despite his silence I had the feeling that he wanted me to follow him. So I did.

The snowfield was veiled in a pale blue light, and seemed to go on forever. The footprints I had made the day before had disappeared without trace. We were heading in the direction of a misty grey forest. The forest was waiting for us like a huge bird spreading its great wings.

We went deep into the densest part of the forest. No footprints were visible, neither animal, nor human. There was a thin strip of sky visible above us. There was the usual dull light, the sun reflecting from the low mass of cloud.

Suddenly, the view in front of us opened up, and we found ourselves in a wide clearing. Dead shrubs were sticking out of the snow here and there. The wind had dropped and we could hear nothing at all except the sound of our own breathing.

He was wearing fewer clothes and was not even wearing a coat on top of his jacket. I followed the back of his boots to the right across the clearing, and went into the conifer forest again. There was no path this time and we stumbled between the trees, in places the snow came up over our boots.

There was a sky peeping in to the forest intermittently between the heavy conifer branches drooping down. The snow was quietly absorbing the faint sunlight and the cold spiralling air.

Hoping that it wouldn't start snowing, I struggled after him. The hem of my long coat became heavier and heavier as it dragged on the snow.

'Are you taking me to see the fir with the star on it? Is that where we're going?'

'It doesn't exist any more,' he said repeating what he had already said.

We came to the edge of the forest. Between the black trunks of the firs, the greys and whites of deciduous trees began to appear. The leafless trees stood like brooms, it was much brighter here, and the tips of the branches were trembling slightly. The frozen air whistled past us. My guide pulled his fur hat down over his ears. I did the same.

The forest turned into a sparse woodland, and the trees became shorter and shorter. Eventually we came out into a huge snowfield through which a few shrubs which I didn't recognise, were poking through. He looked from left to right trying to get his bearings. Finally his gaze settled on a point in the far distance on the right, he started walking in completely the opposite direction. I followed him looking back towards the direction he was staring at many times, but there was nothing to be seen other than a dense grey forest and above it a heavy bank of snow clouds. When he caught me looking behind us, his eyes suddenly flared with anger. He glared at me, apparently angry that I might try and find my way back here. I went back to following his footprints, my eyes on the ground ahead of me.

After a while the trees disappeared behind us, as did the forest in the far distance which he had been staring at. Everything disappeared from our sight. Other than the vast snowfield and the low snow clouds covering the sky, there were only the two sinful humans spoiling the purity of the earth. Perhaps his sin was his belief in God, and mine, that of no longer believing. But the fact that we were here at all in the middle of this perfect whiteness seemed proof that this earth, this snowfield had already forgiven.

I was beginning to think that it didn't matter whether or not I ever saw the fir tree with the star. My body was so tired it was refusing to go any further and was ready to lay down and go to sleep. The faint brightness in the sky had already disappeared and a weak wind was dragging at the two pairs of feet crawling across the frozen snow. I had looked at nothing other than my feet for a long time. Neither to the left, or to the right of me. Nothing. I was worn out. And I cursed myself again for coming here.

Suddenly, he stopped walking. I looked up to see a strange wooden monument in front of me. When I caught up with him, I was out of breath.
'What happened to it?' I asked.
'It's been burnt.'
'What has?'
'A fir tree.'
Even colder air touched my cheek and flew away.
'What do you mean? Was it struck by lightning or something?'
The tree was about six foot high and there was snow and ice piled up where the top had been ripped away.

'It was struck by a cannonball.'

'Pardon?'

'A civil war .'*

'Why here?'

'Well, this area was one of the battlefields. It was a tragedy. Many thousands died here.'

'Really… And where was the fir tree with the star? Is it far from here?'

He ignored me, and began turning back along the way we had come. Two lines of foot prints were drawn in the snow.

'That was the tree.'

For some reason I felt no surprise, perhaps, because my emotions were drained from fatigue and cold.

'So the star at the top must have been smashed to pieces, I suppose?'

'Well, I never actually saw the tree when it had the star on it, to be honest. I just heard from the hunter that this was the one.'

'Ah, I see.'

* After the Russian revolution in 1917, anti-revolutionary forces continued fighting for about three years. It was during this time that a British force landed at Murmansk and Archangelsk to support them.

Strangely enough, I didn't feel like looking back at it, but just walked side by side with him feeling quite calm. I cannot remember how long we walked, but when the hut came into sight, my bag was waiting for me at the entrance. The innkeeper was out.

The unwelcoming mood he had shown at the beginning had now disappeared, and he made me a warm cup of tea with the hot water in the kettle. He looked relieved somehow. And asked me,

'How do you know the story of the fir tree with a star? Did you hear it in a nearby village?'

'No, in fact you probably wouldn't believe me if I told you. It's just something I've known for a long time,' I answered. What else could I say?

'All the village folk know the rumour. But they haven't come here for a long time. The greedy ones took the story of the silver star literally and came here to try and find it. Ridiculous. I've had enough of the whole thing. I gather you're not one of them though.'

'I just wanted to see it once, but it's ok, I can understand why something so old doesn't exist anymore.'

'Did you here of it a long time ago?'

'Yes.'

'Who made up the story? Do you know?'

'I do, but don't you think there is a secret world inside

your mind which you never tell anyone about?'

'I do indeed,' he said smiling.

Somehow, he seemed pleased by what I said. I sensed he had his own secret world inside his head, and that was very important to him, but it was something he could never share with other people.

'Are you going back to the station to get a train?'

'Yes, I am.'

'Then I'll give you a lift on my sledge. It looks as though it's going to start snowing again soon.'

I thanked him for the offer and got on the sledge.

We began to move off across the fine powdery snow. The sledge was pulled by two horses with shiny coats. It picked up speed very quickly, and the inn soon became a small speck in the distance.

We came to a snowy gentle slope, then, down a small dip, and up another hill. There was a grey forest stretched with no limit in a far distance on the left. There was no change in the view no matter how far we went. I got bored with looking at the unchanging landscape and was trying to remember Yan's story. And with the fatigue from yesterday and the warmth of the furs wrapped around me, the memory became a dream, and the story became a poem. And as I drifted towards sleep, my consciousness began telling the story, desperately trying to reach the end, before I fell asleep completely. The beautiful story which only I know...

Section 2   The Celebration in the Meadow

I The First, or Autumn Journey

i) A ticket for a Sentimental Journey

The sky was so clear from edge to edge it was almost sad. I closed the door quietly behind me and began climbing the slope, stepping carefully to avoid the thistles. In the valley below me, the river was snaking slowly through the grassland, leaving lakes as it went on its way.

The ginger-coloured stripes on my back glittered gold as they caught the light, reflecting it back to the river. The gentle wind flattened my fur and a few wisps of hair drifted away on the breeze.

When I reached the top of the hill I turned and looked back. The grass I had walked over showed the path I had taken all the way back to the hut. The thistles and pincushion flowers on either side were swaying gently in the breeze, as if wishing me well. It was a wonderful feeling.

Over the hill, the path went on, through grass, and more grass. At the bottom of the slope were a few huge boulders, lying where they had come to rest at the end of the Ice Age.

After a while I looked back but all I could see was the silhouette of the hilltop and the sun going down behind it.

Further on I came to a granite outcrop and sat down to eat the cabbage pirogi* which had been swinging around in the net bag by my side. The view was magnificent, a primeval, elemental landscape.

A pine forest covered the land as far as the eye could see. Here and there were a few open clearings, like islands in a sea of treetops. From up here, you would never know there was a railway running through the forest.

I walked down the lower slope, a grassy meadow where a few silver birch trees grew, then breathing the resinous scent of the pines, I went into the forest. I followed what seemed to be a well-worn track leading deeper into the forest. By then the sun was too low to reach the path I was following.

* Pirogi: a kind of big pie-like thing made from various different ingredients and served baked or fried. For example there is cabbage pirogi, meat pirogi and fish pirogi too. Small pirogis are called 'piroshki'.

Yan on the hilltop

The shadows of the trees were beginning to darken the tracks as a train came puffing up from the South. A line of passenger wagons clattered by, then some goods wagons, then a postal carriage. I jumped up, onto the train and watched the pine forest going past and the hilltop receding into the distance. There is always something lonely about watching a landscape passing. When it goes by slowly you notice flowers sprouting beside the rails, or a silver-birch tree growing against the darkness of the forest on either side. Then as the train gathers speed, it becomes like a stream of memories going past.

'When you board a train,' as The Pike once said, 'you are buying a ticket for a sentimental journey.'

And this particular sentimental journey is one I have taken before.

It was a journey in search of a distant childhood memory. That ramshackle old town of Savinski was the source of all my memories. A town of farewells, and of chance reunions.

When I feel especially lonely, I step up onto that train without even thinking.

Each letter of the sign up there on the front of the station:

'SAVINSKI', that basement room in a street on the edge of the city, distant footsteps, a shadow in the doorway of the storeroom where the sacks of coal and potatoes were stored…

All these images come swirling back to me, unable to surface clearly amid the turbulence of everyday life, like grains of sand spinning in a jar of water.

The train stopped at a deserted station, having past several others equally deserted where nobody got on, or off, or sighed at the beauty of the twilight. Scraps of weeds clung to the wheels of the train as they began to turn quietly. The ticket-office was overgrown with creepers. Behind the station was a wasteland of dying grass, littered with a few dead trees.

The train began to gain speed, as if trying to erase the deserted station from memory. I stared out at the field, lulled by the regular rhythm of the train running over the tracks. The telegraph poles flickered past. The wire between them carrying messages from my subconscious.

I was on the verge of sleep.

ii) Savinski

The platform was lit with orange lamps. A few elderly women were selling their wares. I passed an old man in a hat who was drinking vodka, and went into to the station café. I picked up a spoon and a glass and went back outside. One of the old women was wearing a red floral scarf, she had a basket of eggs on her arm.

'Eggs. Fresh eggs.'

'I'd like an egg,' I said.

'Well Mr Pussy Cat, have you got any money?'

'Er, no I haven't.'

'Well in that case, you're supposed to say: 'May I have an egg, please?'

'Er… Could I possibly have an egg, please?'

'Alright Mr Pussy Cat. Here you are. Take it,' and she handed me a nice fresh egg.

I broke the egg into the glass and began whipping it up with the spoon.

Further down the platform was another old lady. She was wearing a blue floral scarf and was selling honeycombs.

'Er… Could I possibly have some honey, please?'

'Well Mr Pussy Cat, have you got any money?'

'Er, no I'm afraid I haven't.'

'Well listen Mr Pussy Cat, in that case, you're supposed to say: 'I'd like some honey.''

'Er… I'd like a little bit of honey please.'

'Alright, then. I'll put it in here,' and she put a nice spoonful of honey into the glass. I stirred up the egg and the honey. By the time the train had reluctantly trundled down the platform, the egg and honey mixture was all frothy. It had become gogol-mogol*. How sweet and delicious it was! I felt much better straight away. I went back into the café, where I left the spoon and the glass on the table, and walked out of the station.

*Gogol-mogol: a Russian dessert like a soft meringue.

Stirring gogol-mogol

From the square in front of the station, an orange glow shone from the station doorway. Behind it, the station itself was a black silhouette.

By now it was so dark that you could no longer see the metal sign saying: 'Savinski' that was up there on the roof. The Town Hall, the Theatre and the hotels that surrounded the square were shrouded in darkness. Lights were on in a few of the windows.

There were several little streets leading off the square. I picked one at random and began walking along. It was an avenue of poplars and, as I walked beneath them, a few stray leaves came drifting down.

The faint fragments of memory that come sometimes to mind, seemed to fade when I came face to face with the things themselves.

'Where are you heading, Mr Pussy Cat?' said a rat, as I was turning the corner of small brick building.

'Well, nowhere in particular really. I was just reminiscing.'

'Were you? But this town is full of sadness for those who are lonely.'

And with that, he disappeared into the darkness.

I decided against turning into the side-streets after that and continued along the main road. By then I was beginning to feel rather sad. I walked on a bit further until I came to another dark building on the corner of the street. I thought perhaps I'd turn the corner here instead. But just as I did so, a little voice behind me said: 'Excuse me again, Mr Pussy Cat, but where are you heading?'

I turned round. It was the rat again.

'Well I'm not actually going anywhere in particular,' I said. 'I'm just wandering around really.'

'Are you. Well there's nothing in this town but sadness.'

And he disappeared off into the darkness.

Each time I came to the corner of a street, the rat was there beside me. And each time, he said the same thing.

'Where are you going Mr Pussy Cat?'

'This town is full of sadness.'

Meeting the Rat

'Where are you going Mr Pussy Cat?'

'This town is full of sadness.'

'Where are you going Mr Pussy Cat?...'

I found myself repeating his words as if in a trance. For the next two days, as I wandered the streets, the words went round and round in my head. I could find no connection at all between what was memory and what was real, and feeling strangely isolated I decided it was time to go back to my hut in the meadow.

The buildings in the square were there to greet me, their outlines stark in the bright morning sunlight. The light is different here.

The station building was still asleep with no sign of anybody about.

In the waiting room on the corner of the large hall, was a middle-aged man with a bulging suitcase which he had tied up with string as if he didn't want his past to spill out, and an old lady with two enamel buckets in front of her, one of potatoes and another of onions.

The café was still closed. As I peeped in through the filthy glass-pane on the door, the light from the tall window shone down on the table, lighting up a solitary wild flower embroidered on the white tablecloth. The glass and the spoon I had left on the table three days before was nowhere to be seen. Someone must have cleared them away. I remembered the sweet taste of the gogol-mogol with a slightly guilty feeling.

There was a bench at the end of the platform by the three silver birch trees which grew in front of the café window. I sat down on the bench, to wait for the train, dangling my legs and tail. Across the track, the yellow leaves of the woods glittered in the autumn breeze. The clear blue sky made me feel inexplicably happy. Being able to give yourself up to the slow drift of time is a travellers' privilege. As I looked up, the light filtering down between the leaves was so bright I had to close my eyes. After a while, the faint image of a distant train was being projected on the inside of my eyelids, and just as it did so, the real train mysteriously appeared silently on the horizon.

There it was, the engine advancing with frantic piston movements, and the carriages dragged along behind it, began to slow down and stopped. No one got off, and only myself, and the man and the woman who had been sitting in the waiting room got on.

Yan waiting for the train

The train gave a jolt and began to move off. I watched the three silver birches, and the café. Then, I saw a kitten stretching to look intently into the café through the dirty window with its paws on the window ledge. The boxes the kitten was standing on were stacked up carelessly and looked rather wobbly.

As the train left the station I glanced round at the other passengers. The old lady was looking down at her buckets of potatoes and onions and, across from her, the man with the battered hat was staring vacantly out of the window.

The rattling got louder as the train built up speed. A bank of clouds floating far away were looking at us from the same position. But the telegraph poles and silver birch woods were speeding up like the frames of an old film gradually blurring together.

When the train approached the deserted station a few stops later, meadows and woodland started appearing. After a while, the trees became sparser. The grass swayed in the morning breeze which rippled through it. There in the middle, with the ripples of grass swirling all around it, was a young fir tree. But immediately, it was hidden behind the belt of forest, and all I could see were the flickering trunks of silver birches and conifers.

Soon the train had to slow down in order to climb a small hill, and I was able to jump off the step onto the grassy bank alongside the railway.

I retraced my steps through the forest, and across the sloping meadow that led to my hill. The granite rocks were standing upright in front of me, their shadows stretching out over the grassy slope diagonally in the sunlight. I was out of breath climbing up the slope. I passed the place where I'd eaten the pirogi.

As I felt the autumn breeze on top of the hill, I wasn't sure whether that lonely town of Savinski really existed or whether each building, and everyone who lived there, the rats scuttling around every corner, the old lady who sold eggs, and the one who sold honey had somehow abandoned everyday reality and now existed only in another realm.

But even then, the melancholy of the town still lingered in my heart.

II   The Second Journey, or Winter Journey

i) The Iceboat

The end of autumn came quickly and winter was soon knocking at the door of my hut. The crystals of ice made the ragged cloth that hung over the window look like a fine net curtain.

After a few days the cloudy white sky disappeared and I was eating hot soup, totally entranced by the thin layer of icy snow glittering with reflected light. The big river, still not yet frozen, lay glinting quietly in the sunlight. It looked perfectly still, as if it was a piece of long silver paper stuck on the earth.

A large bird which was late migrating flew past at the level of my eyes with its wings spread wide. The landscape it looked down upon was covered with snow and freezing earth, and there was frost on the branch of the tree it was about to perch on.

By mid-December, the rabbits in their pure white winter coats, the grey wolves, and silver foxes were able to go skating on the big river. On a sunny day around Christmas, everyone scampered outside to play in the thin transparent air. I wanted to go outside too, but I'm rather shy when it comes to things like that, so I just watched from the window of my hut.

It was also a bit of a shock to see my old friend, The Pike sealed in the river beneath the thick ice.

I realised I was on the verge of sinking into a bout of depression.

'I know,' I thought, 'I can go to see what the town looks like at Christmas!' and decided to go back to Savinski again.
 It was quite a warm day for December, but even so, as I walked out of the hut, I was wearing my felt boots, a pair of woollen gloves, a scarf and a hat with ear-muffs. I didn't bother taking any food with me because there wasn't really anywhere to stop and eat it on the way.

There was hardly any snow on the slope of the hill. I was wrapped up so well I soon began to feel quite warm. Too warm in fact. But further down the slope the snow was frozen on the path. In some ways I wished I had come here on a really snowy day.

As I went through the meadow the silver birch trees rustled their leaves in welcome. The meadow was as dreamlike as ever. I stood there, looking at the trees and the wide open spaces between them, as a feeling of deep calm spread over me. Far off in the distance was the shape of my hill, like a mischievous grey hat.

The treetops were sprinkled with cotton-wool-like snow. There were ranks and ranks of fir trees. The narrow path between them was half hidden in the snow. The footprints of adventurous creatures like rabbits and weasels crossed the path and went into the forest. Deep in the forest where the sunlight never came, their footprints were frozen, sealed forever in the whiteness. A frozen reminder of the moment they had scampered across the path.

When I see footprints like these on the pure white snow, I feel tempted to follow them quietly into the forest and stay still there forever. But resisting the temptation, my felt boots added their own tiny prints to the others on the path.

The single straight track railway heading off through the snow seemed to be a small, defiant attempt by humanity to impose something of itself on this vast white wilderness.

I felt uncomfortable being in a place where humans and nature were competing against each other.

The train came, puffing out great clouds of white smoke. The noise of the train echoed out over the canopy of the forest causing the snow to slip from the conifers as if it was frightened of being absorbed into this world of silence.

I jumped up onto the step of the carriage and opened the door. Inside it was another world. The heat of the fire brought back the feeling of the warm spring air. The train was almost empty. A bright-eyed old lady who looked a bit like a chicken, and an old man who looked like a skinny cow were sitting facing each other looking at the snowy view of the conifer forest out of the window.

As I walked up the aisle, I was stopped by a blond man with a turtle-necked jumper who sat at the end of the carriage.

'Hey Mr Pussy Cat! Why not sit here? Where are you off to?'

'Thank you, I'm going to Savinski.'

'You haven't got a ticket, have you Mr Pussy Cat?' he gave me a cheeky smile.

'How can you tell?' I asked him, rather taken aback.

'I haven't got one either, Mr Pussy Cat,' he laughed again.

'Haven't you? And, where are you going?' I asked.

'I'm going all the way to the end of the line, to a port on the Northern Sea.'

'Does this train go that far?'

'Yes, to the very edge of the earth. I'm going to pick up an iceboat, there.'

'So, you're a sailor, are you?'

'I am indeed, a second mate to be preicise.'

'Is the Northern Sea really as magnificent as they say?'

'It is indeed. We have to carve a course through the ice. Huge rocks of ice float along behind the boat, and when you see such deep blue and that layer of ice above it, you get a glimpse of eternity.'

As I listened to him talking, I had a vision of a line of enormous blocks of clear blue ice floating behind the boat reflecting the deep blue wake of the ship. The beautiful surface of the sea was without even a ripple, and there was only a single beautiful canal dug through the endless field of ice.

I could picture the wavering course of the boat as the bow crushed its way through the ice. That narrow crack in the ice, which was all that was visible of the pitch-dark sea and the sheer frightening depths beneath, gave me the feeling I sometimes have of the world around me.

'But, listen, after a whole day, the ice closes its gap. Occasionally, even an iceboat gets trapped in the ice when the weather is unbelievably cold.'

'And what do you do when that happens?'

'There's nothing you can do. Except wait… for the ice to

melt. But, if we've waited a while, and it looks like it's not going to melt, we have to abandon the ship altogether and head off across the ice by dog-sledge, till we get to a town or settlement somewhere.'

The story of the ice in the north went on to the comfortable jolting of the train. I was tempted to stay on the train and see the sea of ice too. But the solitary harshness of the landscape didn't appeal, and the Siberian huskies who dragged the sledges put me off altogether.

I often think dogs are more down-to-earth creatures than cats. Their eyes never stare off into the distance. All they see are their owners' gardens and the next door neighbours', or the fence of their farms at most. Even when they do seem to stare, they don't just stare, they always seem to be looking at something in particular. Only eyes which stare at nothing in particular can hope to catch a glimpse of eternity.

And before I knew it, the sledge-dogs had brought me back to the real world.

'So anyway, I was travelling by dog-sledge… Oh, is my story boring you? By the way, the sledge dogs are very hard workers.'
'By 'work', you mean 'work for people, don't you?'

'Of course.'

'They don't work for themselves, do they?'

'Well no, but, they are given a lot of care and affection, and the choicest fresh meat.'

'Mmm,' I said doubtfully. To be honest I was no longer interested in what he was saying.

'Don't you think dogs are very down-to-earth creatures?' I said.

'Well, that's because humans who own them are down-to-earth people,' he replied.

'Yes, that could be the reason,' I said again, aware that I was being somewhat persistent.
'That could explain why dogs that aren't owned by humans, like stray dogs for example are less down-to-earth. But they can't survive that way for long.'

'Being 'down-to-earth' is not about whether we can eat or not. There are always one or two dogs wandering aimlessly about, aren't there? I mean the ones that sometimes wag their tails to people, and then disappear quickly… I like them because they don't see things with down-to-earth eyes.'

This time I was aware that he was not listening to me. Talking to humans was always like this in the end. We both stopped talking quite naturally and sat staring out of the window.

The frozen signal posts flying past meant that we were nearing a station. We must have passed that deserted station some time back.

All that was visible now was a large expanse of snow, where there was a single leafless tree with snowflakes on the end of its branches like a broom, and a solitary rook standing vacantly beneath it.

the rook beside the tree

ii) The Decoration of the Galaxy

After a while, the train pulled into Savinski Station and waited silently.

The three silver birches spread their delicate bare branches in front of the café window. The bench outside had a thin covering of snow that was beginning to freeze. The window was so steamed up you couldn't look into the café but the light glowed brightly from within.

I almost slipped as I got off the train while saying goodbye to the sailor. The cold air I'd temporarily forgotten clung to my fur and wouldn't let go. And the sky was a layer of thick grey cloud. The old ladies who were usually selling their wares were nowhere to be seen.

When I looked into the café through the half-open door, the man I'd seen drinking vodka on his own in the autumn was putting a forkful of marinated herrings into his mouth. The inevitable bottle of vodka was there in front of him. At another table, a middle-aged man and his wife were eating Chicken Pozharski Cutlets, and an elderly couple were eating kidneys in Madeira sauce. There were also two middle-aged men drinking together, another was eating fish soup with rye bread, and an old man with a pair of thick glasses, who had an enormous long-haired dog by his feet, was eating some sort of hors d'oeuvre with hard-boiled eggs.

An aged violinist with an old hat and a scarf was playing Moldavian gypsy tunes. Strands of cigarette smoke wafted across the room, and the echo of bored voices competed with the clatter of knives and forks.

There were about fifteen tables laid with pure white tablecloths, although they looked as though no one had sat at them for a very long time. Having shaken my tail, I plucked up the courage to go inside, and sat down at a table near the man drinking vodka. There were no waiters around, though even if there had been, I knew they wouldn't have paid any attention to me. I suppose it was a bit impolite of me to go straight into the café still wearing my hat with its big ear-flaps.

When I got my breath back, the man drinking vodka and I looked at each other. He motioned me to go over. Reluctantly, I went over to his table. He pointed at the two left over bits of marinated herring and pushed the plate of towards me. I pointed at the plate and then myself because for some reason, I felt I had to keep silent. The old man nodded, and, he seemed to be smiling a little for a moment. He also gave me the glass of untouched water that stood in front of him on the table. I thanked him politely and carried the plate of herring and the glass back to my table.

When I looked round, he'd gone back to drinking the vodka. The scraps of herring were very vinegary. While I was drinking the water, holding the slippery glass carefully with both front paws, the aged violinist came to my table and played a gipsy tune*- the original version of Zigeunerweisen by Pablo de Sarasate. I was amazed at how beautiful the tune had been before it became well known. The simple melody spread its melancholy ripples across the empty café repeating the same refrain over and over again.

I gave a little stretch, and with my eyes I said goodbye to the vodka man and left the café just as the enormous long-haired dog was wandering slowly over to sniff me. In the central hall of the station a lady carried on knitting an endless scarf one end of which was wrapped round her neck while the other hung down to the floor.

Outside the station, it became even colder and the road was now frozen. The buildings around the square appeared to be shivering with cold. Only the entrance of the theatre was lit up, the lights shining on two posters. One of which said

*A famous Romany tune, also known as 'Gold Earings'.

eating pickled herring

'The Snow Maiden by Alexander Nikolaevich Ostrovsky. Music by Pytor Ilyich Tchaikovsky.'

As I looked back from the middle of the square, the steam wafting out of the entrance of Savinski Station froze at once, and turned into an icy fog. Then, it was swirled up into the air, and was blown up into the sky before settling as ice, on the letters of the sign: 'SAVINSKI'.

I crossed the square and came to the avenue of poplar trees where I had been in the autumn. A few snowflakes started falling. Although strangely neither the town, nor the sky were dark. For some reason, my mind was far from melancholy. My spirit was light and so were my footsteps.

The memory I had carried with me didn't seem to matter anymore. This was reality, and here reality took the form of each brick stack neatly upon the next, to make the old buildings which in turn made the town itself.

'Everything is OK just as it is,' I understood.

There was no preparation for Christmas nor signs of any kind of celebration at all. Just as before there was no one about. The pavement was covered with a thin layer of snow and I took care not to slip. At the third crossroads, I saw a few people for the first time. A group of them were buying some fir trees. They were all wrapped up well in their coats and one was buying a fir tree which was about the height of a child. When the customers had all gone, I went up to the tree-seller who was wearing a cap.

'I don't sell to cats,' he said curtly. His jacket was threadbare and was covered in patches.

The lightness in the air disappeared, and heavier snowflakes started falling straight down quietly. When I looked up, I could see them spiralled down towards me. One after another they came out of the dark emptiness and landed on my eyelashes and hat with earmuffs. I was mesmerised by their beauty for a little while. My fur was soon covered in snow and I had to brush it off with my paws.

As I walked down the gentle slope past several crossings, I caught sight of the rat I had seen before walking towards me from the street on the left.

Eventually he noticed me.

'Hello Mr Pussy Cat, where are you going?'

'I'm just wandering about,' I said. 'I wondered what this town might be like just before Christmas.'

'And what is it like?'

'Nothing really changes here, does it? Except there was a man selling fir trees at the crossroads back there, but as soon as he saw me he said he didn't sell to cats. That upset me a little. But never mind.'

meeting the rat again

As I was speaking, he hesitantly hauled a small fir tree onto his back and looked slightly embarrassed. I had the impression I'd said something clumsy, but to be honest, I hadn't noticed him carrying the fir tree until that point. I was actually thinking what a coincidence it was that we had met again.

'I'm sorry to hear that,' said the rat.

'This town can be lonely sometimes,' he added, and disappeared off down an alley.

The fir tree he held had already been decorated with a few silver moons and stars which caught the light in the darkness.

As I went on, I thought I saw those silver stars and moons glinting far off in the distance. But it was hard to tell whether it was actually Mr Rat's tree because it was so far away.

As I walked on again, I thought I saw a rook walking towards me on the other side of the street. It was hard to be certain because his dark silhouette merged with the darkness, but from the way his shoulders were hunched over it looked like a rook.

As he approached, it became clear that it was indeed a rook. I was slightly surprised to see that he too held a small fir tree under his wing. I passed him, glancing at it occasionally as he drew closer. The rook kept on walking silently with his head down. His fir tree also had a few small stars and moons and with each step he took they caught the light as if they were dancing.

There was a thin layer of snow on top of the rook's head. Where on earth did he get hold of the fir tree?

Further on, an old lady wearing several coats was selling decorations. In the baskets in front of her were moons and stars made of silver paper, bells in green and gold, and red and white Father Christmases. There were no customers.

When I looked into the baskets, the old lady poked her face out of the coats and said,
'I want to sell everything and go home. No one comes in this cold weather. That rook a little while ago was the last one. Can you see anything you would like?'
'Yes, several things. I could go on staring at them for ages, but I have no money.'
'Never mind. Which one do you like? That silver star?'
'Yes, it's very beautiful, isn't it?' I sighed.
'I wonder why silver things are always so popular?'
She muttered, threw several stars, moons, bells and balls into a paper bag, and gave it to me.

the rook carrying his tree

'Er, I have no money. So, I'm quite happy just looking at them,' I said quickly.

'Don't worry.'

She pushed the paper bag into my paw and stacked up the baskets. She lifted them on her back like Father Christmas and started hobbling away.

'Thank you so much!'

I called after her.

The old lady gradually disappeared down the street.

As I looked down, there was a single silver star on the floor where she'd been standing. It was reflecting the street lamps so brightly that it looked like a real star that had fallen from the sky onto the frozen pavement. I picked it up and brushed the snow off it with my paw. I put the star into the bag with the others and peeped inside. The moons and stars were jingling together.

Now that I had such beautiful decorations I began wishing I had a tree of my own to hang them on. But, I had no money to buy a tree and even if I had, I didn't want to buy one from the man I'd seen selling them on that street corner.

I found myself becoming rather envious of the rat and the rook going home with their trees. Anyone with the space to put up a tree and decorate it must be a happy person. But not everyone has a place where they can do that. I myself am only passing through this lonely town. I imagined them arriving back home with their trees and finding all the Christmas preparations well underway.

The street suddenly became narrow and I felt the pressure of the buildings on both sides as if they were leaning towards me like something out of a cubist painting. I decided not to go any further and instead I went down a dark little ally on the left. The alley twisted and turned, and most of the windows had the shutters closed and the rest had dim lights inside.

After a while I came to a dead-end. I assumed that if I turned left again it would bring me back to the station. Then an orange glow caught my eye. It was coming from a basement window on the right of the cul-de-sac. There was a silhouette of a small fir tree and around it were several rat-like shadows. I was drawn to the window and peeped inside and saw what seemed to be the same rat I'd kept meeting before and several of his children standing around the tree. When I knocked on the dirty window they all turned round. Then, the rat noticed it was me and opened the door.

'Hey Mr Pussy Cat! What are you doing here?'

'What a coincidence!' I said

'Perhaps it is?' said the rat. 'This town is a sad place. I think you'd be happier if you went back home.'

'It is sad. Isn't it? By the way, is this way to the station?'

'Yes, it is. If you go to the end of this street you'll come to the square in front of the station.'

As the rat finished speaking, several fireworks went off, shattering the silence and momentarily lighting up every dark corner of the alley. The red, yellow and white lights flashed on the basement window making the baby rats' eyes shine beautifully like small gem stones pressed against the glass.

'Those are the fireworks of that businessman, Schtoltz.'

Then another firework shot up from the other side of the alley, but it was just a single firework.

'Oh, that must have come from the nobility, that's Oblomov's estate over there.' The rat explained to me kindly.

And then the short-lived fireworks ended as if they were illusions. 'I'm sorry that I can't invite you in,' said the rat looking guilty, 'but it's rather chaotic preparing for Christmas with all the children. They're orphans, you know.'

'Not to worry,' I said. 'We'll probably meet again sometime. Goodbye, then.'

'Goodbye. Look after yourself.'

This time, it was his turn to watch me disappear without

being able to scuttle off into the darkness as he usually did. After all this, my hope of sharing the jolly mood of the town just before Christmas seemed rather empty, and as I hurried home I was feeling sadder and more lonely than I had in the autumn.

But even so, I felt a gentle glow when I thought of the paper bag held tight in my paw, and of that chance meeting with Mr Rat preparing his home for Christmas.

The snowflakes which had been falling steadily downwards began floating on the light wind. They spiralled amongst the buildings and never seemed to settle on the ground no matter how long you waited.

By the time I reached the station, the snow was dancing wildly in the station square. Then it turned to a blizzard. I stood against a pillar at the station entrance, watching the sky above the square, my face poking out of the scarf.

One after another, snowflakes would fall out of the darkness into the light of the street lamps, before being blown away by the winds. After a while, it was hard to tell whether the snowflakes were really falling or whether I was floating, and the snowflakes were still like the stars in space.

There was no sign of people and the theatre entrance was dark. 'Snow Maiden' must have ended some time ago. Only the posters showed up in the orange street lights, the corner of one of them flapping in the wind. The row of poplar trees I had passed on my way in were obscured in darkness. It was impossible to follow the row with my eyes now that the street lights were fading in the blizzard.

When I entered the central hall of the station, the same old woman was still knitting her scarf in silence. The scarf, which now wrapped her neck in a few more layers, looked very warm. My own scarf was threadbare by comparison, though the thought had never occurred to me until then.

The café was closed but the light had been left on, and through the window I could see the white of the tablecloths, and the black of the wooden chairs. Having nowhere else to go, I decided to spend the night in the waiting room. I sat down on the carved wooden bench. Fragments of what had happened during the day were projected here and there on the walls of the hall. I fell asleep watching them, overcome with fatigue.

In my dreams, Mr Rat whispered, 'It is sad here,' and the rook walked passed me silently with his tree under his wing. The tree-seller who said 'I don't sell to cats,' was putting all the unsold trees onto a bonfire. The flame dwindled and the snow fell steadily. The old lady who sold the decorations stumbled on, leaving a trail of stars, moons, silver strings of tinsel, from a hole in the sack that she carried. A whole new galaxy of stars was being born in her wake.

iii) The Short Story Writer

The train sped towards the station in the morning light. It was cloaked in the hard, cold arctic air, and was running about an hour late. I was woken up by the noise of the train and the squeaking brakes, and headed for the platform.

There was nobody getting off here. At least, nobody left the station. A man in an expensive fur coat with steamed up reading glasses and a walking stick came down onto the platform, holding the handrail as he went down the step. He could have been just trying to kill time while the train was at the station, or perhaps he wanted to observe the thin morning light you get in these high altitudes.

The man glanced at the three silver birches and at the café. When he noticed me, he came closer and with a faint smile on his face, he said, 'Well, Mr Pussy Cat, is that paper bag your only luggage? It's good to travel light isn't it? I must say this station's rather run down isn't it?'
'No, it isn't. It just looks sad now because it's early. But later on there are old ladies who sell eggs and honey, and then there are rats and rooks who come here.'
'Is that so?' nodded the man in a rather patronising manner. I noticed there was frost on his moustache.
'By the way, Mr Pussy Cat, that paper bag you are clutching

so tightly is wet and looks as though it might split any minute. What have you got inside it?'

'Are you a detective or something?' I said.

'Ho, ho, ho. Well, the reason why I'm so nosy is because I'm a humble short story writer. I can't help being intrigued by all kinds of things. And a cat holding a paper bag is not something you see everyday – so that's why I asked. I had no wish to offend you. Please forgive me.'

'A short story writer, eh?' I replied, rather unimpressed. 'Well, as a matter of fact, all I have in my bag are a few silver stars, and moons, and things like that.'

'Ah, that's beautiful. To hold the universe in this one small bag? What a magnificent poem that is!'

Then, a very glamorous lady tugged the frozen train window open and shouted, 'Antosha*, you'll catch your death of cold out there. Come inside at once.'

*Anton Pavlovich Chekhov (1860-1904). Chekov wrote a letter claiming that he was staying in Nice in December of this year, but in fact he was here in Savinski. Olga was an actress. She married Chekhov the following year.

'Here we go. Well, Mr Pussy Cat, what are you going to do with the small universe? I expect you're going to decorate the tree in your nice warm room, am I right Mr Pussy Cat?'
'No, they won't sell trees to a cat.'
'Hmm … So what are you going to do, then?'
Then the lady shouted again,
'Antosha, please! What are you going to do if it gets worse? Moscow is still miles away. And I can't even bear to think about Yalta. It feels like an eternity! Anyway, come inside!'
He paused to cough three times – it seemed to me he looked a little in pain.

'OK, Olga. I'm coming. And please don't shout so loud. You'll frighten Mr Pussy Cat, here.'

His face was lit by the lamp reflected on the blue ice covering the platform. It looked very pale though perhaps that was just the colour of the light. At that moment, another gentleman came out onto the steps and said,
'Antosha, please come up, quickly. I beg you.'
'Standing out here is bad for my piles!'
The kind looking man on the steps shouted jovially,
'Uncle Vanya!*
We must live! We must go on living, Uncle Vanya!'

*Chekhov's play 'Uncle Vanya' was first performed in October 1899. It was directed by Nemirovich Danchenko.

'Alright, Nemirovich. That's enough. I'm coming.'

Their theatrical conversation was too much for me. I climbed up the step and went into the next carriage along. It was nice and warm inside. The carriage seemed to be empty. I walked along to one of the seats in the middle, took off my hat and sat down. Then I noticed someone sitting in the seat to my right.

A rook was staring blankly out of the window, watching the trees. They looked like a stack of upside-down brooms. Brooms with frost-silvered branches. On the seat next to the rook was a fir tree bigger than he was. A few stars and moons hung limply from its branches.

I wasn't sure whether it was the rook who had passed me on the road, or the one I'd seen from the train standing in the middle of an empty field. From a distance they both looked black and depressed. This one had spiky feathers on the top of his head.

The carriage where myself and the rook were sitting, and the adjoining one with the theatrical group (of course, there were several other carriages as well), were hauled away by the reluctant engine and we finally left Savinski Station.

After a while we came to the vast snowfield. The single tree was still standing alone in the middle. Although this time

the rook on the train

there was no sign of the rook I'd seen there before. I couldn't help turning round to look at the rook on the train. He seemed to be asleep with his beak down on his chest. The stars and moons on the tree beside him were jolting to the relaxing rhythm of the train. I wondered where he had boarded the train and where he was going to get off.

The train rattled on. But the carriage where myself and the rook were, and the one with the writer and his friends, were going in different directions even though they were joined together. In the end, the train drifted away altogether and the carriages floated off silently like thin clouds in the bright summer sky. I could see only endless snowy moors and sparse leafless silver birch trees. The meadow where we lay in the summer, or the roots of the silver birches with yellow leaves in the autumn seemed to be dream worlds we had imagined all along.

The train was crossing this vast canvas drawn along by the intermittent whistle and black smoke of the engine. On the horizon, layers of grey conifer forests appeared and disappeared. Then, just as the fir forest and silver birch trees merged, it turned into one vast snowfield. The feeble sun appeared from the south-eastern horizon and travelled over miles of forests and snowy hills. When it reached the snowy field I had to close my eyes. The light kept dancing wildly in my closed eyes.

After a while, when it calmed down, I opened my eyes slowly. The train was at the deserted station. As usual no one got on or off the train. Snow was frozen to the wall of the station and made it look like a house made of icing sugar. Then the light crept over it, and it was transformed into a winter palace.

Shortly after the station, a young fir tree in the sharper sunlight caught my eye from the gap between forests. I remembered that day in the autumn when the same tree stood on its own in the middle of a rippling meadow. A rustling noise brought me back to the present. I peeped into the paper bag I was holding tight. The stars and moons were crowded on top of one another in the small bag.

'That's just the tree for my celebration!' I thought to myself. I could put the decorations on that little tree standing there all on its own in the vast, sad snow field, and then they would catch the thin winter light and bring a golden glow of happiness to the whole field.

I was delighted by my new plan and turned to glance at the rook. At that very moment, the rook, who had either been dozing or staring out of the window, suddenly looked straight at me. And unusually for a rook which spend most of their time moping around with their shoulders hunched, he smiled cheerily, as if hearing my thoughts and wishing me well. I smiled back at him.

When I looked out of the window to see the fir tree, it was nowhere to be seen, hidden by the snow-covered trees of the forest. For some time after that I kept looking into the bag, telling the moons and the stars about the idea which had suddenly came into my mind. I told them I had found the perfect setting, and that they would soon be playing the leading roles in the scene I had imagined.

I waited until the train reached the slope and began chugging slowly uphill, then clutching the bag tightly in my paw, I jumped. But as I landed, my foot slipped and I fell flat on my face in the snow, scattering stars and moons all around me.

The bag was all wet and now had a big hole in it, so I took off my hat with the big earflaps, picked up the decorations and put them inside. While I scrabbled around in the snow, the train chugged away up the hill carrying the rook and his fir tree off into the distance.

Then, I climbed up my hill carefully holding the hat with the stars and moons inside. I was able to climb quite easily because the snow was firm, perhaps because it was colder than when I left. Eventually I reached the hut, and opened the door, exhausted.

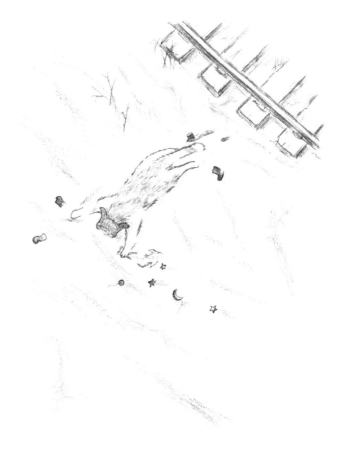

Yan falls in the snow

The room was soon filled with the warmth of burning twigs. I looked down at my hat, at the moons and stars resting quietly.

Then while staring at the condensation on the window, I began dozing and found myself daydreaming about a single fir tree decorated with moons and stars standing on its own in a vast snowfield. Above me, the night sky was filled with millions of stars like those on the tree. The beauty of it completely took my breath away, all I could do was stand there entranced beneath the tree. Just like the rook I'd seen from the window of the train.

III The Third Journey, or the Journey in the Blizzard

From dawn on Christmas Eve, the sky was covered with snow clouds, although fortunately there was no wind. It was time to carry out my plan. I wrapped the paper stars and moons in greaseproof paper so they wouldn't get wet and put them in a cloth bag. Then putting the bag over my shoulder, I went out of the hut.

I struggled down the hill and was waiting for the train when the snow started falling. It was light at first, but by the time the train arrived, the wind had got up, and the snowflakes were streaming horizontally against the front of the train. I jumped aboard, and the train was soon racing down through the conifer forest.

The weather was getting worse. All I could see through the patch of window which I'd wiped with my paw were countless snowflakes spiralling in the strong wind. I sat staring at the space with the bag of stars and moons on my lap. Now and again I wiped the window with my paw but all I could see was snow. After a while the window itself seemed to become bored that it was unable to show anything of the outside world, and began reflecting the interior of the carriage instead. That was even less interesting, just those empty rows of hard wooden seats.

There was no sign of the rook today.

In most places, people would be getting ready for Christmas parties, waiting for the moment when midnight comes and the festivities begin. Some would be going to church. Thinking back, I realised I hadn't seen a single church in Savinski. Perhaps it was like a town in one of those landscape paintings where a few people are shown for effect, but you can't make out their faces. They're just standing there on the canvas, trapped and lifeless. But wait, you can just make out the slight movement of the rat. At the far end of a darkened alley some time after sunset, an orange light glows from a basement window. A party is being thrown for the little orphan rats of the town. And there they are, singing carols to themselves.

The snow crystals melted as one by one their brief lives came to an end. As I looked at my reflection in the window the snowflakes were swirling all around me.

For one brief moment I thought I saw the rook reflected in the window, but when I looked round he was not there. By the time we arrived at the deserted station, a blizzard was blowing.

Yan on the train

A stream of ice crystals stung my face. Everything, my hat, my gloves, and my whole body, was covered in snow. It was impossible to see any distance, and soon I could only see a few steps ahead of me. Reluctantly, I stopped.

In a blizzard like that even The Snow Maiden would have had a happy romance.

The blizzard had hidden the fir tree completely. It also covered me, turning me into a snow sculpture of a cat. A cat holding a bag. I shook myself, and all the snow fell to my feet. The wind went right through my fur, it was bitingly cold.

My little dream had failed miserably.

Although at that moment I was too worried about the cold to have any thoughts of failure or loneliness.

After all that I ended up spending Christmas Eve on the train going back home. The blizzard outside was showing no sign of letting up, and it was still impossible to see a tree or anything else out of the window. The silver stars and moons were sleeping in the cloth bag on my lap. They were free, no one could disturb their astronomical will, even God could not disturb them.

But what about the real stars in this severe blizzard?

The blizzard comes
One star falls
Then another

I picked up the fallen stars and put them one by one into the bag with the other stars and moons. In that tiny cloth bag I was holding the whole night sky.

IV Constellations in the Drawer

The Christmas and New Year celebrations were over all too quickly. I was no longer disappointed that I didn't have a tree of my own. The old year seemed to drift into the next without any feeling. Thinking back, it may have been the uncertainty about what lay ahead, like a young officer about to set out on a new mission; writing the dates of January on the first page of his new journal, and then noticing for the first time that he was at the beginning of a new millennium. The year was 1901.

The curtain of the new millennium rose like this. My hut just about withstood the severe cold of January and February. March crept by ever so slowly and at long last the ice began to look as if it was beginning to melt.

I pulled the desk drawer open to look at the stars and moons the old lady had given me in that bleak December town. And when I rattled it shut, they formed another set of constellations. They seemed to be moving of their own accord just like the real ones in the night sky.

It was Easter by the time the snow had melted completely. And by then I'd forgotten about Christmas altogether. In May, the first pale yellow and blue flowers began to appear

the constellations in the drawer

in the meadow I can see from my hut on the hill, and trembled in the chilly wind. As I looked from one to the other I could follow the course of the meadow stretching away into the distance.

One day, as the breeze carried strands of fur across the big river, the summer began. All the animals had longed for the summer. The foxes, the quails, the squirrels, the herons, and the finches, all were delighted. But they were too shy to show it. They would pass by you on a path and as you turned round, they would turn round too, their faces filled with glee that summer had finally arrived.

I spent some beautiful summer nights in the meadow in front of my hut, looking up at the stars that covered the whole sky. I watched the shooting stars appear and disappear. Even after they had disappeared I could see them, their paths of light superimposed on top of each other, like memories.

Night after night I watched the stars. I spent a wonderful time all by myself. The grass, the hill and the universe belonged to me. As I lay on my back, the heavens seemed to pause for a moment and every star stayed where it was, twinkling. It was as if each star was pinned up there, or hanging by an invisible thread.

Then I remembered the young fir tree out in that blizzard in December. It was the first time I'd thought of it for a very long time.

The borders between constellations are only imaginary, man-made things.

A long time ago, The Pike was complaining that there is no constellation called, 'The Pike' although there is one called 'the Fishes'. But it doesn't bother me that there is not one called 'the Cats'.

Each of the stars is up there on its own. It is only man that joins them together, to make the shapes he wants to see.

… the train was picking up speed as it followed the railway north. The autumn wind must already be blowing in the port town where the railway ends and the Arctic Ocean begins. The weeds on the clifftop were trembling with the cold wind from the sea. But despite that, the waves coming towards the land were surprisingly calm and there were hardly any white crests on them.

A timid-looking young dog was running around aimlessly wagging its tail frantically. The dog couldn't keep still, and ran off towards the end of the headland. As he disappeared from view, a group of dark grey clouds came across the sea from the North Pole and covered the whole town.

An old white cat was sheltering from the cold wind behind the houses at the top of the lonely bay. There seemed to be something wrong with his eyes, as though they were diseased in some way.

I asked the cat if his eyes were sore.

'Not at all,' he answered.

It suddenly became dark because of the clouds.

I asked him if he could see.

'A little,' he said. 'But then having good eyesight is not so important in a town where it's dark half the time.'

The raindrops started slanting diagonally in front of my eyes and gradually hid the cat sheltering beside the house. The rain pattered down on a rusty tin plate that someone had thrown by the wayside. I went down to the quay. There were no boats moored there. The raindrops were vanishing into the sea.

Lots of silver paper stars and moons came floating across

the sea towards me. They swirled in the rain, and were washed inland till they came to rest on the shore at the far end of the bay. I picked them up and brushed the mud-like black sand off them. I thought of all the times I'd picked up stars and moons in the past…

As I was watching the distant rising sun I shivered in the cold air and realised that summer was coming to an end. It was the first time I'd felt lonely all summer. I decided that the time had come to decorate the fir tree. So that the stars and moons do not have to go on being scattered around the world. And I do not have to go picking them up.

The plants in the meadow were wet with the morning dew. As I lay down, the leaves of the cranberry touched my paw. The small red fruits were already beginning to appear. They were magnified through the lens of a dewdrop. After a while the morning mist came from the bottom of the hill obscuring the morning sunlight, and a pale pink haze covered everything from view.

the cranberry bush

V The Fourth Journey, or the Journey at the End of the Summer

i) The Frozen Moment

A couple of days later, the fog became thinner, and glimpses of pale light lit the meadow. I gathered the stars, moons and bells into a basket woven with silver birch twigs which I then put inside the cloth bag.

The descent from my hill at the end of summer was fun. I scampered down past clusters of cobalt flowers and some others which looked like lace flowers peeping out between the blades of grass. Then I stood beside a silver birch, staring at the different shades of deep green grass which shone in the light coming down through the trees. A train came chugging up, bringing with it a fresh gust of air.

I jumped up onto the steps right at the back of the train and watched my hill receding into the distance until it was hidden by the tops of a silver birch trees. Seen from this angle it was more like a steep cliff rather than a hill. Everything, including the conifer forest and the silver trees on both sides of the railway, seemed to be enjoying the late summer. The glittering lights, coming through between the trunks of the trees flying past, shone on my fur. The ends of my fur shone gold, and flickered in the breeze.

Looking at my fur, it reminded me of the dart-like yellow leaves of larch trees as autumn was approaching. The yellowing of larch trees is one of my favourite things as well as that of silver birches and aspens.

I opened the door into the carriage and was surprised to find several people sitting around in silence. Face down with their eyes closed, or deep in thought with their chins in hands, but none of them seemed to be enjoying the day at the end of the summer.

'What kind of strange wind has brought you here?'

It was the sailor of the ice-boat who I'd met on the train before Christmas.

'The gentle autumn wind,' I answered.

'Oh yes, of course. It's sad that the summer's coming to an end, but the meadow's still green, isn't it? And the trees have still got their leaves.'

He looked much older than when I'd last seen him. It was less than a year ago and yet now there were streaks of grey in his blond hair. I realised how tough his job must be to have caused him to age so much. I thought of the lonely bay, the port, and the remote headland which I'd seen in my dream.

'Are the sledge dogs well?'

I'd only asked because I couldn't think of anything else to talk about.

'What? Oh, the dogs. Yes they're as boisterous as ever, barking all the time. That's all they seem to do.'

'Is it?'

'Where are you going, Mr Pussy Cat? Savinski? Not a very lively place, is it? Anyway, are you going to stand up the whole way? Why don't you sit down?' he said pointing at the seat in front of him.

I'd been standing up to watch the meadow going past the windows. But we'd almost reached the end of it now, so I sat down. I put the bag carefully on the seat next to me.

'I'm getting rather tired of being on the boat,' he said. 'We always get trapped in the end no matter how much we break the ice. We get stuck... although you can put the engines into reverse and edge back a little into the past. But after a while, even that becomes impossible. There's no escape. Think of this meadow as the ice field. At the moment the train is going forward but after a while, it will be impossible to go either forwards or backwards. We can't go forward in time, and we can't go back. So we try to live in the present, but we can't even do that. Here, the present is still breathing, but in the middle of the ice even the present stops breathing, the breath freezes instantly, and there is no air to breathe in. So the whole universe becomes trapped in one brief moment of time.'

'And if we are content in that brief moment, don't you think that is the secret of eternal happiness?' I asked.

He was silent, his chin resting on his hands. He let the telegraph poles go past for a while and said,
'Unlike animals, we humans are unable to live in the present for any length of time. Even if we can stop thinking about the future, we can't go on living if there is no past to go back to. You say you're fine if there is only the present. But the present is filled with images of the past and the future. If the present was completely disconnected from the past and the future we couldn't stand it,' he mused to himself.

'Can you animals really live in the present moment, without the past and the future?'

'Of course, our instincts are attuned to the present.' I answered with confidence.

'Just as a gull breaks the crests of the waves with its wingtips as it takes off, so we can live by feeling only the peak of the present moment.'

'So, you have no sense of history?'

'No, there is no need for it, is there?'

'Although it may not be necessary, you inevitably find yourself thinking about the future built on top of the foundations of the past, don't you agree?'

'But these 'foundations' - what use are they really?'

'You mean to say they should be pulled down and replaced by something new?'

'No. Is there anything worth destroying to be replaced by something totally new in your world? Of course, there isn't. Not in our world. Values and foundations never really existed in the first place. Our world is merely a continuum of pure consciousness. If you don't believe me, cut the world in two, and tell me what you see?

 - the grasses, and the blue and white flowers waving in the wind. The birch leaves flickering in the breeze. Some lose the will to cling on and fall before they have had a chance to turn that beautiful shade of yellow. The sunlight is highlighting the silvery-white of their bark and making their black stripes darker. The grasses by the side of the tracks sway as the train goes by, and then the leaves drift down, burying the railway, hiding the scar where the train has passed.'

Suddenly, there was the sound of the train going over the

points and the deserted station approached as if it was flying towards us.

'I envy you, Mr Pussy Cat.'
'No, we are all the same.'
'Goodbye, Mr Pussy Cat.'
'Take care.'

I stood with my bag of stars in my hand and watched as the train went away. There was a smell of iron coming from the brakes, and as this drifted away, the trees rustled their leaves in welcome. The sound of their rustling led into the forest and tempted my mind to follow after it.

The deserted station was bathed in a pale green light from all the vegetation that had grown up around it.

Yan on the track

ii) The Other Christmas

While the train trundled away behind me I started walking along the bank of the railway. There were woods of silver birches and other green-leaved trees near me and beyond them the dark conifer forest. The tips of the fir trees, visible above the birch woods, were swaying elegantly in the wind. Silver birch leaves rippled when the wind blew through them. The grass swayed slowly around my feet, gently touching my fur.

I went to the edge of the birch woods where the meadow began. The meadow was like a grassy sea lapping against the bank where I stood. And there in the middle of it was the little fir tree standing apart from the others. I went down the bank of the railway towards it.

It was truly wonderful to see my fir tree with the late summer sun upon it as I waded through the tall grass. But, it was further away than it looked. The bank of the railway was buried in the grass when I looked back. I noticed that the meadow went slightly uphill.

When I reached it I could see that the young fir tree was slightly taller than I was. The short grass around it felt nice and soft on the soles of my paws. As I looked back, all I

decorating the tree

could see was the meadow, with the conifer forest on either side. Here and there I could make out the silver-white trunks of the silver birch trees against the black of the fir forest. The meadow itself seemed to go on forever. What was needed was a line to show where it met the sky. So, trying to keep my paw steady I drew a line across the vast expanse in front of me.

When I'd finished drawing the borderline between the sky and the meadow, I took the silver bells, stars and the moons which had rolled out of the cloth bag, and one by one, I hung them on the tree. I took the basket out of the bag and there were still a few decorations left. I tied them neatly on the branches so that they wouldn't be blown off by winds. Already, the stars were spinning, the moons were swaying, and the bells were swinging without making a sound.

It's a fiddly business tying threads and some of the decorations had already came undone and fallen off. So I had to keep picking them up and tying them back on again. Finally, I put the biggest star on the very top. Eventually, after a great deal of effort, I finished decorating it and the little tree looked splendid. The silver stars and moons shone out against the dark of the branches. I walked round and round the tree, looking at it from various angles, it was wonderful to think that such a small fir tree was able to hold the whole universe and all the stars.

Yan and the christmas tree

The western horizon turned from red to gold and for a brief moment, the silver decorations caught the gold of the late summer twilight, and reflected it back in farewell.

The forest, the hills and valleys lost their colours, the light faded and the dark came suddenly like the darkness in my hut when the lamp is switched off. Stars began appearing all over the night sky. The stars of the whole universe twinkled quietly around my little tree.

I felt... This moment stands on its own. A moment without past, without future, without even the present.

A faint breeze stroked my soft fur and stirred the bells on the tree. But there was no rustling sound from the treetops or the grasses. The absolute world. All religious experience, all worship, and all the most profound philosophies... all fell short of this. Even the moment of quiet prayer was lost.

'An absolute world' – that was how The Pike used to discuss his poetic theory, always going on about it with his wet dorsal fin reflecting the lamp. I would sit there nodding off, just counting how many times he used the phrase, 'the absolute world', (usually about ten) and just staring at the way his mouth opened and closed.

And as we sat chatting together, I thought that *this* moment, the present was indeed 'absolute'. It was more beautiful than any poetry, painting, or music, especially The Pike's poetry – in fact, to be honest, his poetry was rather unsubtle – and his theories too, come to that.

I lay down on my back on the grass. The stars had started to turn in their orbits with the tree at the centre. The tree looked very tall. And the silver paper star at the top was shining even brighter than those in the night sky. The tree merged into the darkness. A pleasant drowsiness came over me, and as I drifted to sleep there were various scenes appearing and disappearing inside my eyes.

The same old man with the violin in the station café at Savinski was playing that tune again, muttering something to himself with the collar of his patched jacket turned up. And that kind old solitary rat and his orphans were sitting on the grass around my tree. Then, I saw the rook standing there staring up at it. The violinist was playing an aria* on his violin. 'Have mercy on me, my Lord' he sang. I shook my head as his eyes met mine. He stopped singing and disappeared from my vision. The violin was left and carried on playing the tune.

*The Aria from 'St Matthew's Passion' by J.S.Bach

I have no need to be forgiven, no need of God's mercy. We have no sins. This meadow is a place for those who know loneliness and feel some sense of sadness for nature, and for the universe… Mercy, jealousy, hatred, and salvation, have no place here.

I drifted off to sleep beside my tree, beneath a sky full of stars.

It was the last night of summer.

The night of The Other Christmas.

the night of the other christmas

VI The Fifth Journey, or the Journey at the Beginning of the Winter

i) The Miracle

A gust of wind blew through the pale blue flowers at the top of the meadow, scattering the faded petals one by one. On each flower the seeds in their cases of soft fur wavered, waiting to fly off to unknown places.

The scratches I had on my toes from the thistles in the autumn had already healed, though now I had fresh scratches on the tip of my tail and on my paws. But the real pain came when I thought of those who always go travelling at this time of year.

Like The Pike for instance. He always seems to become more of a poet when autumn arrives, and would often visit my hut, before disappearing off on some long journey of his own. But not just The Pike. There are others as well. Others who love this golden season and yet are touched by its indescribable sadness. I would often see them wandering aimlessly through the woods or meadows, trying to catch the autumn before it disappeared. I would watch them going off into the distance through the yellowing leaves of the birches, and firs.

Yan peeping from behind a tree

But the autumn always moved faster. And I was left behind, standing in the meadow where suddenly it was winter. I held my paws up to the setting sun to warm them up in the freezing twilight air.

From the far horizon a single beam of light reached my paws. A single beam of light passing hills and forests and meadows.

It was not really a miracle, just something that happened everyday.

the deserted station

ii) The Dance of the Snow

The rain turned to sleet, and the sleet to snow. Then it was
sunny for a few days before the weather turned cold again.
There was a light scattering of snow, too light to stay on the
ground, as I boarded the train once more for the deserted
station. I thought of the fierce blizzard of the Christmas
before. I wanted to see the little fir tree again before the
winter really set in. Then when Christmas came, and I was
stuck in my hut with the blizzard raging outside, I could
think of the tree standing on its own in the vast meadow
decorated with the silver moons and stars.

The light, down-like snowflakes floated aimlessly, seeming
to lack the will to join together. Except when they came
into contact with the train, when they were sucked into
the spiral of the wind created by the carriages and melted
as soon as they hit the windows, or flew off over the roof
snatched by the air rushing along the sides of the train.

The train gradually approached the deserted station while
the telegraph poles flew past one by one with the snow
dancing mysteriously around them. I pushed my nose
against the cold window of the carriage waiting patiently
for a glimpse of the tree in the meadow.

It was only ever there for such a short moment. If I blinked it might be gone forever. And then there it was! My fir tree appeared and disappeared in that brief moment. I closed my eyes and stared at the afterimage. The little fir tree, and a myriad snowflakes held still in the air. The snow seemed to stay there without falling. But I couldn't see the silver star shining at the top of the tree.

The snow was already dancing in my tiny heart.

The train passed the signal pole and pulled into the deserted station. The wail of the engine immediately turned into a cloud of minute ice particles that drifted towards the station.

When I got off the train and stood on the platform, the snow in my heart was falling more heavily, and by the time I was walking along the railway, it had become a blizzard. But the real snow was still floating down dreamily.

When I reached the meadow, patches of black earth were visible here and there. My fir tree was standing there sadly in the middle of the vast expanse. The snow was dancing even more merrily. And there was definitely no star on top of the tree. I climbed up the slope feeling anxious and slightly out of breath. I looked all around for the star but could see no sign of it.

I sat down by my fir tree and looked round in all directions, at the conifer forests, and at the silver birch woods which were leafless now. Above them all was the infinity of space. The snow was dancing in the air but there was no sign of it settling. Occasionally a snowflake would almost touch the ground but would then be distracted by the faint wind blowing through the dead grass and would fly back up into the air again.

I lay on the dead grass to watch the dance of the snow. A whole universe of snowfakes was falling from the sky. I turned my head, to look at the fir tree, and hanging by a tangled thread from one of the branches, was a silver moon.

The snow had turned to fog. It became slightly warmer and the dampness clung onto my fur. I went down the very slight slope leaving my tree with its silver moon.

On the way back I found the silver star lying on the slope. It must have been blown there by the wind. I picked it up and looked back, but the fir tree was already hidden in the fog and I couldn't even see where it was.

Yan lying on his back

iii) The Sculpture of the Rook

I was standing at Savinski Station as darkness fell. A misty
rain was falling on the platform. The gas lamps had already
been lit. Neither of the old ladies were there selling things.
The track leading north was hidden in mist, only the glow
of a lantern was wandering. I peeped through the café
window, the old man who gave me the herrings last
Christmas was sitting on his own, drinking vodka. He
picked up a gherkin, popped it in his mouth and wiped
his hand on the hem of his grey jacket. Another old man
in a large coat and thick-framed reading glasses was there
too. His shaggy-looking dog sat by his feet looking up at
him. The man drinking vodka seemed to feel me watching
him and glanced towards me. I nodded and he seemed to
smile back but I might just have been imagining this.

Inside the station, the melancholy sound of a violin was
drifting through from the entrance of the café. It sounded
a little like Brahms's Hungarian Dance, but it wasn't a tune
that I knew. I remembered seeing him in a dream, playing
the violin under a tree on a summer's evening. But I had
turned away. I felt sad now, even though it was only a
dream. As I went past the café, the sound of the violin
merged with that of the aria and turned into an
impromptu duet.

Savinski station

In the cold empty space of the central hall, an old lady in a red scarf was busy picking the sprouts off potatoes. She still had another bucketful waiting for her. By her feet was a basket of eggs. The basket was woven from silver birch twigs and the eggs were stacked up neatly, all nestling together. They reminded me of the taste of that gogol-mogol from last autumn.

I went out of the entrance of the station, the wet cobble-stones were glistening in the misty rain, reflecting the street lights. The town hall, the theatre, and the old hotel, which formed the other three sides of the square were shrouded in mist. I could barely make out their shapes through the misty rain.

Why had I come back to this town? This place didn't hold even a fragment of the memory I was searching for. Well this would be my last visit then. As the thought occurred to me, everything became even sadder. I felt the stone wall where the theatre posters had once been. When I brought my nose close to it there was still a faint smell of old paper. Then I stood against the wall and stared at the misty rain falling on the square. There was a light just above my head and I was lit up like one of the stars of the theatre posters. I felt a little awkward. Just then, the rat stuck his head out of the theatre entrance beside me.

outside the theatre

'Hello, Mr Pussy Cat, what are you doing standing there?'

He had said more or less the same thing the first time we met.

'Oh, nothing in particular, but the poster…'

'Ah, the play is still on even though there are no posters up.'

'Really? Then this theatre has been open all the time?'

'Yes, Chekhov's new play has just finished. He was here, too. It was quite interesting.'

'Was it?'

'Yes, but then this town is still lonely after all.'

He came out with his usual phrase and trotted along the side of the square before disappearing off between the poplar trees.

But even though he scuttled away out of sight, he could not escape altogether from my memory. As I watched him disappear, the image of an enormous rat-shaped balloon, inflating and filling the whole square, suddenly appeared in my mind.

I looked up at the dark sky again. The misty rain simply appears; it is impossible to witness the moment of its birth.

Around the square the streetlights were spaced at regular intervals and above each one was an orange glow, like

an enormous rat-shaped balloon

candles in a holy place. But, for me there was nothing to pray for. At this very moment, here in this world, all that exists are the lonely Station of Savinski, the buildings surrounding the square, myself, the streetlamps, and the cold misty rain. No, wait I've forgotten something. At this very moment, from that same row of poplar trees where the rat has just disappeared, a rook is about to walk into the square, hunched over as usual with all the sorrows of the world on his back.

I decided that today I would finally talk to him. He came into the square and unusually for him, he looked up and stared at the misty rain falling for a while. The spiky feathers on top of his head were now squashed flat with the rain. And the feathers on his back were reflecting the streetlights in a rainbow of colours.

Just as I was going to go over to talk to him, he looked at me. His face looked very calm and seemed to be smiling. I just smiled back, and what happened next was unbelievable.

He spread his wings and with only three flaps of his wings he was up on the top of the station roof, perched on the letter k of 'Savinski'.

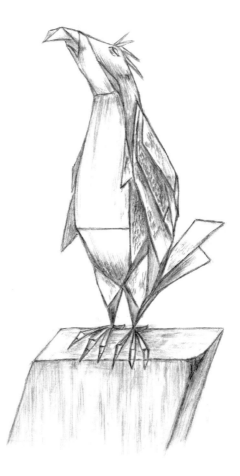

the rook on the letter K

He looked very majestic perched up there, a far more imposing profile than that of a hawk or even an eagle.

I felt I understood this town at last. There was nothing I needed to search for here. I walked round the square once and went back into the station passing directly beneath the rook.

When I looked back, the misty rain had turned to particles of ice. It was beautiful, as if a crystal chandelier had been shattered to pieces.

I waved goodbye to the old lady who had fallen asleep whilst picking the sprouts from the potatoes, and went out to the freezing platform. Before leaving I peeped into the café. There were a few customers, and the violinist was playing the same tune over and over again. It sounded like a gipsy song called, 'Gold Earrings'. The vodka man was cutting some marinated herrings into small pieces and giving them to the kitten I'd seen before. The kitten was sitting on the chair facing him and looked very content.

The train pulled into the station with its usual deep sigh. I stood with my hand on my chest to say my last farewell to the station and the town behind. It was a grand, and rather theatrical gesture, but then I loved this town and station dearly.

Yan saying farewell to Savinski

The train jolted forward and then back before moving away at no more than walking speed. I grabbed the handle and jumped onto the step. Behind me Savinski Station, disappearing in the darkness, was reduced to a few orange lights through the sleet. The tip of my nose stung where the small hailstones hit it. Despite this, I leant out of the step and watched the lights of the station, which became a speck in the distance until it finally disappeared altogether. An orange speck that glowed so brightly onto my eyes that it would never be completely erased.

iv) The Writer and a Crane

I entered the carriage, and to my surprise there were several groups of passengers. Each of them was daydreaming the usual human daydreams. I walked forward between seats.

'Oh, you're the cat I saw some time ago,' said a voice behind me. It was the writer I'd met last year.
'Yes, I thought so. You're Mr Pussy Cat, aren't you? We met last winter.'
'That's right, we did.'
'Why don't you join us? You'd be very welcome. I was bored because I had no one to talk to. This crane doesn't talk much. Then again, there's not much left to talk about.'

A crane was sitting next to the writer on the window side and looking at the monotonous vast field. I sat down, somewhat reluctantly, and as soon as I did so, he smiled and began firing questions at me.

'Now let me see... I remember, Mr Pussy Cat, what happened to your small universe? You said you couldn't buy a tree. I remember that much, very clearly. Well, what did you do after that? What happened to those silver moons and stars?'

'They fell off. All except for one moon.'

'Did all the stars fall off?'

'Yes.'

'Really? That's a shame. I suppose you had to put them all back on again, did you? Or, did you decorate something else with them? Never mind. Where did you hang them?'

'On a fir tree.'

I was so irritated that I wanted to wag my tail, but I was sitting on it so I twitched the end of it.

'Oh, so you did find a fir tree. (Cough.) Excuse me. That's good. That must have made your room all bright and glittery. Well, Christmas makes us excited no matter how old we are. Even an old man like myself. Even I think, 'Oh, it's Christmas again!' But what is it really like? I mean is the animal Christmas, well, different from the human one?'

'From the outside it's just the same. But it's more humble somehow. We celebrate quietly for ourselves.'

I was looking at the crane's neck. I was thinking that it was too long. In fact,… well,… the whole body of a crane was out of proportion.

'But you don't go to church? For Midnight Mass and things?'

'No, because we don't have a God.'

'Oh, you mean, you don't believe in God?'

'No, because God does not exist in the first place.'

the Crane

'Then, why do you celebrate the Christian Christmas? Surely for you it's just the same as any day of the year?'

'Yes, that's right. We started because we were imitating human Christmas - because the decorations were so romantic. As you say, there is no real need to stick to the day at all. We do that just out of habit. And because we can.'

'I see.'

I got bored with looking at the crane's neck and tried to look out of the window as the crane was doing. But, it was pitch dark outside and it was impossible to see anything other than the very occasional hail stones hitting the window. I wondered what the crane was seeing in the darkness.

I became aware of my face reflected in the window. It was a contented face, no sign of disappointment or discouragement. I looked at the crane's neck, and then the reading glasses on the writer's nose again.

'Well, let's change the topic. Is it true that you animals act from instinct or intuition and don't have introspective thoughts? And is that why you feel that God does not exist?'

'Well, you haven't really changed the topic at all. But never mind. We do have thoughts, too. But we use our intuition more often than humans do.

By the way, instinct isn't the same as intuition. Instinct is the primitive form of intuition, and is the key to understanding nature, the world and the reason for existence itself.

So intuition is dependent upon instinct. Then thoughts come afterwards.

You humans decide there is or isn't a God on the basis of thought whereas we understand things more instinctively.'

'So, God never existed from the beginning… ?'

'That's right.'

There was no hail hitting the window any more. The crane wiped the window with its wing and tried to look out, but there was not a star to be seen.

'But if a country was governed purely by instinct and intuition, wouldn't it just become a world of fear and desire?'

'Perhaps in the human world. But instinct and desire are two different things. Humans often confuse the two, but instinct is intrinsically beautiful, and intuition is a fleeting vision of instinct, and that is the most beautiful thing in the world!'

'So Mr Pussy Cat, you prefer intuitive beauty (cough) to speculative philosophy (cough), am I right?' asked the writer leaning towards me and coughing a little.

'The division is a little strange. In your philosophy there are a lots of clever arguments which are trying to capture that beauty. But I don't particularly mind you forcing that logic on me.'

The writer leant back against the seat and crossed his legs the other way round.

'I agree on that point. So, what do we end up with…? A shrine to beauty. And even that is half-rotten and a great wind is blowing across it. (Cough.)
Mr Pussy Cat, I understand a half of what you are trying to say. (Cough.) But… the other half… the world of beauty… the meaning of existence… novels and plays are…'

I'd got bored of chatting with the writer and my mind drifted off. The images of the crane and the writer became super-imposed and the writer looked gaunt and frail. Then the image of the crane, holding the stick and with the reading glasses on his nose, appeared. The crane carried on looking out of the window without saying a word. His feathers looked cold on the outside, but the inside which were visible here and there looked far warmer than my fur.

I would love to drift off to sleep in a feather as soft as that…

I was woken up by a jolt, probably the train going over the points, the writer and the crane were both asleep with their necks bowed down. The writer's face was very pale. While I was asleep, the train had passed the deserted station some time back and was about to reach the bottom of my hill. As I wiped the window and looked out, there were many stars in the sky.

I said farewell to the crane and the writer without waking them up, and jumped off the train. I was surprised at the freezing cold air outside, but the moon was so clear that it was easy to see around with the moonlight.

With the moon and the stars to guide me, I climbed the hill and reached the hut which was cold, and empty, and tired of being left abandoned.

V The Pike

i) The Arrival of Spring

So life went on and the New Year came again and still my little fir tree had no decorations – well, perhaps there was still one moon hanging from a thread.

The New Year festival which the forest animals celebrate secretly was somehow irrelevant for me. The calendar on the wooden wall of my hut still had the row of December numbers with Christmas Day on it for a long time.

But the winter light was changing to the joyful light of spring and the sunlight glittered and danced on the fast swollen river and the marshy pools around it.

Then one morning, the Pike knocked hesitantly on the door of my hut with the golden light of spring behind him.

'It's open,' I said. 'Come on in.'

'Oh, so it is. This door is always open to the world! You see the ice has started melting and the cold air has become warm again, and, well, because my heart opened so very wide, I er, I thought I might go for a long walk… then, I happened to…'

the arrival of the Pike

The Pike held the door open wide, and stood there in the doorway talking. The gentle sunlight outlined his entire body, reached inside the hut, and tickled the white fur on my stomach.

It was wonderful to see him again after so long.

The Pike expounded on the new philosophy which he had come up with while resting under the winter ice, on the questions which he had yet to solve in order to develop it further, and on his own innovative opinions on the direction that poetry should take in the coming revolutionary era. I didn't disagree with him on these but simply took the role of the listener. Then, when the talk had eventually come to an end for a while, and we were sitting sipping tea, I began telling him about my trips to Savinski.

I told him about the ever-lonely Mr Rat, the rook who appeared wherever and whenever you least expected him, the gypsy-violinist who always played the same tunes, the old lady crouching down beside her potatoes, the old man who liked vodka and marinated herrings, the women selling eggs and honey, the old lady who gave me the Christmas tree decorations, the sailor from the ice-boat, the short story writer who asked all those questions, and his crane that never said a word, the station, and the square in the snow, the deserted station on the way there, and a single fir tree standing in a meadow....

And as I talked, my thoughts went back and forth along that branch-line to Savinski.

'Really? I knew that you'd been to Savinski, but you went there again did you? I never knew that. Then again, I've spent all winter under the ice, debating with Mr Cod... He says that after the coming revolution the Animal Kingdom will come into its own. I'm not that optimistic myself, to be honest. We go on doing what we need to do. Pursuing beautiful things... but it's not good enough just to maintain the status quo. We always need to find new ways of expressing ourselves... For example,'

'More tea?'

'Ah, yes, please. So, for example, creating an entirely new system of written language, yes, the Cod language... it's pretty good, it even rhymes...'

'Well, a new writing system is fine, but what's the point if hardly anyone else understands it. The language we already have can be used to say beautiful new things, I think. At least, there is no reason for it to be new. That's what I've been feeling, recently.'

'Well that's right, of course. The expressions themselves don't have to be completely new.
… But, I am a little bit confused myself…'

'Eh, don't you think that there is no need just to stick with poetry or philosophy? For example, you are good at making things, Mr Pike. That umbrella was very well made and extremely sturdy.'

'Was it?'

'Yes. When you are stuck, it helps to do those kinds of things as well. If you are still stuck, it's OK just to stand still and look at what's in front of you, and to think, 'Ah, this is the unfolding of something important,' without actually trying to be creative. It doesn't matter whether it flies past you in a second or if it takes years to go past you. Whenever you see, hear, or touch something, you are in the eternal world and what you feel is unforgettable.'

'Yes, when I think that way I become relaxed and feel my heart opening up. So, Yan, like my poetry and philosophy, you tried to create something this time round as well as seeing, hearing, touching and feeling the important things.'
'Ah, you mean decorating the fir tree?'

'That's right,' he said.

'That was as much as I could do. I wanted to create some small symbol in that meadow.'

'Oh, so it's Symbolism, isn't it?'

'No, there is no need to categorise things and label them in –isms. Even if you define something, it doesn't mean that you have solved a problem or achieved anything. It is just an intellectual exercise. Meaningless. Beauty is related to action. It's not an interpretation.'

The Pike listened to me silently. Sometimes it looked as if he wanted to say something, rippling his dorsal fin.

'You say a symbol of something, but a symbol of what?'

That was the question.

'Well… a symbol of SOMETHING. You know when you see something that moves you – it might be a work of art, or a beautiful scene, or it might just be something very plain, it might even be something you see only in your imagination – but something that makes you say, 'Oh, this is the moment!' – in that instant you have a gentle breeze inside you… Then, that breeze sets off another, and that sets off another, all across the meadow, and gradually they all start spiralling round some centre. My young fir tree is standing all on its own at that centre. The smell of the earth in spring, the fragrance of the flowers floating in the grass in the summer, the sound of the dried grasses rustling in autumn, and the dance of the snow in winter… the fir tree is seeing, hearing and feeling all these things. And I wanted to decorate the tree with the silver moons and stars as a symbol of that.'

'And wasn't it perhaps for yourself as well, Yan?'

The Pike pointed out bluntly.

He was sharp today.

'Perhaps that's true too, but anyway they have all gone now as I told you…'

The sunlight which had been tickling my stomach was already shining on the sooty ceiling reflected by the samovar on the table. My eyes were drawn to the grain in the ceiling. I had never noticed the patterns on the ceiling before which I had just glanced up at. There must be so many things I don't really notice.

Yan staring at the ceiling

Perhaps I'll never notice everything – not even to the end of my days. Perhaps that's the reason for the sadness which is always with us.

'Oh, Yan, in that case, I will make those silver moons, stars and balls. Just hang on a minute. They are very easy to make.'

The Pike's face was fired up with inspiration.

He was itching to start work immediately and before he'd properly finished his third cup of tea, he hopped off down the slope on his tail fin.

Far off in the distance the big wide river was hazy in the twilight. And as I looked down the slope of my hill, I could see from the tiny pale green shoots of grass, that spring had finally arrived.

Yan on the track

ii) The First Autumn Breeze

After that it was a while before I saw the Pike again.

Now and again I would open the drawer of the desk, but instead of the silver moons and stars, and bells and baubles, there was only an ink-pot. When I closed the drawer, the ink-pot rolled over on its side, before settling quietly inside.

The spring rains swelled the river, but it soon returned to its normal level, and from my hut I could see it glinting in the sun all day long. I had no visitors.

The season passed quickly and only my thoughts were left behind.

My thoughts went backwards and forwards along the railway between Savinski and the fir tree in the meadow so often that they began to freeze in the snow. My consciousness was in each droplet of ice on the tips of the branches alongside the railway. Even if I never took that train to Savinski again, my consciousness would lie frozen in the earth between the sleepers of the track, or glint as frost on the weeds between the rails. And when the sun came out, my consciousness would become a thick fog covering the railway and the whole branch-line would disappear.

Yan outside his hut

The sun was pale on the big wide river and the marshy meadows on its banks were shrouded in summer haze. I opened the dirty window gently and sat down to look out of it. The mist crept up the slope swallowing the clusters of daisies and swaying white camomile, and the pale blue harebells. It came right up to my hut. The mist stole in through the window covering the half-drunk cup of tea, and the samovar which was left sticking up out of it like the tower of a cathedral.

It tore off the August page of the calendar, left its damp mark on a page of the book I was reading, and wrapped my fur in its chill. On the opened page of the book there was a poem titled, 'August'.

Then a shower came wandering over. The raindrops pattering on the window-sill. The flowers and their stems were still after it had passed. Grass and leaves were on top of each other soaked in water and trying not to laugh. And when each of them stood up yawning, the sun was stretching its faint light from the horizon in the west, unable to decide whether or not to go down yet.

It arrived all of a sudden. What did? The Pike? No, the autumn wind. The autumn wind knocked at the door drooping with fatigue. I ran to the door, worried about the rattling of the hinges, and opened it gently. The grumpy cold air flowed in, threw a few scraps of leaves on the floor, and began warming itself up. I found myself thinking of the draughts in the winter and hoped the door would fit snugly. I began picking up the yellowing leaves that were scattered around the door, and it reminded me of picking up the silver stars and moons.

A few days later, the autumn wind knocked hesitantly at the door again. Was it just a coincidence? I opened the door a little, apprehensive about the visit of even more cold air. But when I did so, the cold air flowing in around my feet carried a faint smell of the river.

And there was Mr Pike standing in front of me, holding a linen bag.

'It's turned cold all of a sudden hasn't it? summer's over. The river water is much colder, too.

Oh, and, er they're done by the way.'

'What are?'

'Yes, er, those stars and moons.'

'Oh, are they? I'll make some tea straight away. Anyway, come inside.'

As I glanced at The Pike whilst making tea with the samovar, he was sticking his fin inside the rather large bag and carefully displaying the silver coloured stars, moons, and balls one by one. After a while he frowned at not being able to reach the bottom of the bag, so eventually he just shook the whole bag upside down. The rest of the decorations, together with some rusty wire and a fragment of an iron plate, spilled out onto the floor.

'Oh, dear. I am sorry. What a mess I've made!'

Despite what he was saying he looked very pleased with himself, and was obviously very proud of his work. It must have been a far more fiddly job than that heavy umbrella he'd put so much effort into making and lent me some time ago.

Whilst sipping hot tea we stared at the constellations of shining silver spread on the floor.

They were not the stars that were washed up on the northern beach, or those moons that were scattered when I fell from the train, or that galaxy leaked from the old lady's bag, or those sad stars that were shaken off the tree at the beginning of the winter. Here they were spread out on the floor of a warm cosy room and I thought perhaps this was where they should stay.

'But Yan, you must decorate the fir tree with these,' said the Pike suddenly.

the Pike empties out his bag

'I would feel inspired to write lots of new poems imagining these stars and moons reflecting the light of the setting sun, and the moonlight. But, as you said yourself, Yan, the act of imagining, thinking or drawing has no meaning other than the act itself. So, please decorate the tree with them. Then the images of our thoughts, and dreams, and poetry become real things and exist. You see Yan, we must raise the flag of the new symbolism once again. Of course it's different from human symbolism, yes…, different, completely different… For those of us who are not a part of the human world…'

He began reading some of his new poems and went waffling on for ages.

I sipped at my tea and stared at the stars, allowing myself to drift in the rhythm of his poems like the ripples on a river.

'I was just wondering… these stars don't look as though they're made of silver paper, but they're not made of real silver, so how did you make them?'

'They are made of real silver. I suspect they're not pure silver, but I stretched them thin and hammered them into the shapes.'
'What? Real silver? But how on earth…?'

'It's Sadko's silver.'*
'What? But that's just a legend.'
'No, it isn't, it's a true story.'

According to The Pike, Sadko was supposed to have thrown silver into the sea as an offering to the King of the Sea. On another occasion he scattered some coins into a river. It was a big river, not necessarily the Volga, it could have been any big river. So, Sadko is not the name of a particular person, but a collective name for all those people who sail in boats like him, and apparently many of them have thrown silver coins and trinkets into the river to pray for a safe return.

'There are so many coins down there that we don't know what to do with them all. Of course, most of them are to be found on the riverbed, in the places where the river flows slowly.'

I decided his story was true because he really was an expert on finding anything on the riverbed.
'Even so, it must have been hard work making them all.'

*The Russian heroic epic 'Bylina', tells how the merchant Sadko became stranded at sea. He made an offering of gold and silver and pearls to the King of the Sea. But this had no effect so he jumped into the sea himself, and consoled him by playing the harp. He woke up to find himself back on the river in Novgorod. These epics are handed down from generation to generation, so there are many different versions of them.

'Oh, not really. I just made a few every now and again whenever I remembered. It's fun making things, isn't it? I could probably have finished them some time ago, but I forgot what I was making them for. I was away for a while over the summer. And when I got back I wasn't sure what all these silver stars and moons were doing on the riverbank. It was a few days ago when the first autumn wind this year came knocking at the door…'

'I would have thought it was more 'the wind knocked hesitantly', wasn't it?' I said teasing him.
'Oh, yes, 'hesitantly' is much better,' he agreed seriously.
Although it was Mr Pike himself who had knocked hesitantly not the autumn wind.

Sometime after midnight, The Pike went slowly off down the slope, moving his fins carefully, as there was no moon or stars to guide him. His figure disappeared into the darkness and soon I could no longer follow him with my eyes.

The air was damp, a sign that the autumn rains were on their way. I closed the door and looked at the stars glittering on the floor. It seemed that all the stars had turned but were still in their constellations. The bells and baubles seemed to have followed the stars. One by one, I picked them all up and put them in the linen bag The Pike had brought with him.

Yan at the window

I've picked up stars and moons like this so many times! And yet, as I picked them up I had the feeling that this was probably going to be the last time. Each of the silver decorations was slightly different, and each bore the signs of The Pike's hard work.

The window-pane rattled quietly to tell me of the arrival of the night breeze. One or two raindrops spattered against the window and trickled off somewhere after following the cross of the window-frame. Then I suddenly remembered that I had completely forgotten to thank him. But perhaps there was no need because, as the Pike himself had kept saying, the stars and moons were a symbol of the world of thoughts we share with those around us including, of course, The Pike himself.

The window rattled again, more loudly this time. But the light of the lamp didn't flicker. It just went on burning calmly.

VIII   The Last Journey, or the Autumn Journey Again

A while after that, I went to the autumn meadow with the silver stars and moons The Pike had made. It really was, – as I say myself – a beautifully sunny day. I got off the train, and took the now familiar path towards the meadow. I soon reached the little fir tree.

However, in my absence, the fir tree had grown a little and I could not reach to put the silver star on the top of it, even if I stood on tiptoe. You're probably thinking that it should be fairly easy for a cat to climb a tree. But the tree was so small I was worried it would not bear my weight. So I went off to fetch one of those wooden boxes I'd seen lying around in the station. I hung the decorations on the tree, carefully threading the thin wires over the branches. Then I climbed up onto the box and tied the silver star to the very top with another piece of wire. A breeze was blowing through the meadow, and the stars, balls, and bells swayed and spun in the wind.

The breeze turned silver and then disappeared. Then another breeze came, and this time, it swirled round and round, dancing with the silver lights.

The horizon was golden. As I looked carefully, I realised it

Yan decorating the tree

wasn't the sunset, but the yellowing leaves of the trees in the distance. A few white clouds were floating above them, almost touching the horizon.

When I had finished decorating the tree, I sat down on the grass on one of the few patches of green that were left. I felt tired, and content, and I felt that this little tree with its moons and stars didn't really belong to me. It was there for everyone, for the Pike, the Rat and his orphans, the Rook, the old vodka drinker, the women selling eggs and honey, the foxes and the rabbits who like skating, the Gypsy violinist, the lady selling Christmas decorations, the kitten in the café, and the old lady with her potatoes. It was for all of them, and for many more besides. It was there for everyone.

As twilight fell, the wind grew cold and it was time to leave. As I looked back, the silver star on the top of the tree was glinting in the setting sun, half gold and half silver. It was more beautiful and more sacred than the cross on the spire of a cathedral.

But at the same time, it was still only a symbol.

I jumped onto the train, the Savinski branch-line, feeling a secret glow inside.

Section 3 - Epilogue, a Man's Reminiscence from 1934

One day in late August, I was looking out at a landscape of blue sky and deep forests. I was sitting on the badly sprung seat of a train going south on the Savinski branch-line. The ponds and marshes which flashed past were dark green, and the clouds were reflected in them.

I lay down on the seat using my suitcase as a pillow. It was a battered old suitcase tied round with a string, the lock had broken years ago. I stared out of the window. The sky became my entire field of vision, framed by the treetops of the forests and the window frame.

Most of the other compartments were occupied, but there was no-one else in mine. I looked down at my crossed legs, and noticed the black sand on the toes of my shoes. A whole day had passed, but still the sand showed no sign of drying. I was on my way back from a funeral. It had been held at the cemetery on the clifftop above the estuary.

'Wherever you dig around here, all you find is this sticky, black sand,' the undertaker had grumbled as he dug. The grave was too shallow.

'And I can't dig any deeper. Might make it easier for him if he's going to be resurrected!' he said throwing down his spade. The muddy sand was sprinkled onto the coffin and I threw a single white rose on top.

Solovetsky Island was not visible from the top of the cliff. It was nine o'clock in the evening and the sun was crawling towards the horizon still refusing to set. But it would have to set sooner or later. Those who lived in this sad time were buried one by one. And those who were buried were the lucky ones, for many simply went missing.

But today's sky was clear and limitless. Perhaps I noticed it more because of the screen of thin clouds I'd seen covering a grey sea the day before.

The railway crossed a tributary of the Onega river, and joined another line heading into the taiga*. I wonder what sort of life is waiting for us beyond that line of track. The railway carried nothing but violence from the one end to the other.

The only way left for us is to go deep into the forest, to wander the wastelands, and woodlands, and to seek solace among the trees and the flowers, like the separatists**.

*the taiga: the great coniferous forest that stretches from the tundra to the steppes of siberia.

I had not seen such a clear sky for a long time. The isolated clouds I'd seen before were no longer framed by the window.

Why do I feel a sense of release after that burial where any display of human emotion was all but forbidden? Have we given up on everything? On life, the future, creation, destruction even? It was as if a lid had been placed on our imaginations and left them boiling like potatoes and beetroots bubbling away in a pan. And, those who ate them became fat and ugly. But, they could never see this sky I was looking at and feel uplifted by it. Those who rule by terror live everyday in terror themselves.

'Excuse me, is anyone sitting here?' said a female as the door behind my head slid back. I was taken by surprise, and taking my hands from behind my head, I sat up. She had an innocent expression on her face, something I had long since lost, and was holding a leather travel bag.
'Allow me,' I said slightly awkwardly and took her well-worn leather bag, and placed it on the seat opposite. As I did so, I smelt the faint scent of the white rose I had smelled before throwing it into the grave.

**The separatists were a group who opposed the reformation of the Russian Orthodox Church that took place in the mid-seventeenth century. Many of them fled to the forests to escape persecution.

'Thank you very much,' she said, in an unexpectedly bright voice, and sat down. She rested her chin in her hand and started looking out of the window. She was beautiful, and to be honest, I found her presence rather unsettling. To explain why the heart of a man in his mid-thirties was thrown into confusion at her appearance, I should point out that she was young and slender, and had long auburn hair. Her looks were not those of any of the peoples of this region, in fact of anywhere in this country. I found her mixture of Asian and European looks very attractive.

As she stared out of the window, her gaze lowered from the sky, to the forests and to the strip of grass beside the railway. In contrast to the cheerful voice of a few moments before, her expression was downcast. Although perhaps she simply gave that impression because her suit was a sombre dark green.

We glanced at each other once or twice, but I'm not very at ease in this kind of situation, and each time I closed my eyes, and folded my arms.

After opening and closing my eyes for a while, our eyes met again by accident.
'It's very sunny today, isn't it?' I said hesitantly.
'Yes, it is,' she answered.

After a few moments' silence, she said, 'Is that sand on your shoes from the sea? It's very dark, isn't it?'

'Yes it is, yes. It's sand from the estuary of the Onega River. It's like black mud. It doesn't seem to dry very quickly.'

'Can you see Solovetsky Island from the mouth of the river?'

'No, not that far. You can probably see it from the end of the peninsula though.'

'Was is a family bereavement?' she said looking at my arm. I noticed I was still wearing the black armband around the sleeve of my jacket.

'Yes, I've just been to the funeral of my uncle who passed away on Solovetsky Island.'

I thought I might as well tell her the truth. There seemed no reason to hide it.

I knew my uncle had probably been forced to end his life. I even felt like shouting that out loudly.

'Did you, that is ...' she said and fell silent.

I couldn't bear to see her frowning, so I said out loud,

'He was a political prisoner. Or perhaps a philosophical one, which amounts to the same thing.'

She looked even more troubled and said half under her breath:

'Concentration camps, criminals and those who put criminals in the camps, that's what we've become isn't it?' she said frowning.

'I'm on my way back from a concentration camp, too. Not the one on Solovetsky. The one on the outskirts of a lonely town up by the Arctic Sea, on the other side of the peninsula from Onega.'

'So, you...'
I was slightly surprised at her confession, but when I thought about it rationally whatever happens in this country is not abnormal and is justified as soon as it happens, so I told myself again that it was nothing unusual.
'No, my father.'
She said clearly.
'Oh, I see.'
I couldn't think of anything to say.
'I went to see him... He was still alive.'
I could only nod to what she said.

Half of the seats faced forward looking into the future, the rest faced backward, for those who look back at the past. As the train rounded a curve, the light reached over the belt of conifers and shone on her face and her hair. She was looking towards the front of the train, and her eyes were half-closed. I was looking back and, to the side of her face, I watched the last carriage disappearing behind us. I had turned my back on the future but ironically I was heading into it just ahead of her.

'The light is becoming stronger, isn't it?'

'It is, isn't it? We are quite a lot further south now.'

In fact, we hadn't actually come that far. But I felt a sense of relief at leaving such desolate regions behind. On the train we were free to relax, at least until we reached Moscow.

'The path leading to the concentration camp is muddy and boarded over,' she said. 'There is a bay on the left with a row of abandoned houses overlooking the beach. Although come to think of it, there were some sheets hanging out to dry outside one of the houses, so there might be someone living there after all. There was a cat in the shade of those houses, it seemed to be blind. When I stroked it, it seemed to be happy for a while, but then it stretched and slowly walked away towards the beach. I was in a hurry to see my father, but I was also frightened about what I would find. So, I followed the cat for a little while.'

I hadn't really been concentrating on her story until this point, but had just been resting my chin on my hand, and looking into her eyes.

'What happened then?'

'The white cat sat on the shore, facing the sea, with the sun falling on its blind eyes.'

'And then?'

'Then, as we were both looking out to sea, I saw something shiny coming towards the beach. A lot of tiny silver specks. They were washed up onto the sand and I went over to have a look at them. They were stars, and moons and baubles, made of silver paper. Just like Christmas decorations.'

'That can't be true… That's…'

'Oh, I'm Lili by the way. Lili Hodrasi.'

Lili Hodrasi! She pronounced the initial 'H' sound very softly, her mouth narrowed, in an attractive pout.

'What a lovely name! But, 'Hodrasi' is…'

'Yes, it's a Magyar name. I don't suppose you've heard of Magyar. It's in Hungary.'

'Yes, I know. I've been to Budapest.'

'Well I'm from Pecs just to the south of there. Do you know a painter called Csontvary? Many of his paintings are left in Pecs.'

'No, I'm afraid I haven't heard of him. By the way, the story you told me just now, is it true? Or just something you wanted to believe?'

'No, I picked them up with my very own hands. They were covered with black muddy sand, just like that on your shoe. It's true, I washed them in the sea. It's very strange, isn't it? I wonder if someone threw them away and they got washed up. But that should they get washed up there of all places. Very strange.'

'I don't suppose there was a rather timid-looking dog wandering around, was there?'

'How did you know that? There was actually. Quite a young-looking dog. A short-haired dog. It was running around wagging its tail, I watched it for a while but then it wandered off somewhere.'

'And the stars…'

'When I looked round after washing them, the cat had gone.' She took two silver stars out of her jacket pocket and lay them on the palm of her hand.

It was a strange story, but how else could you explain this, for there they were.

'Would you like to have a look?'

As I touched her hand and the stars that it held, I thought back to that night about thirteen years before. That insane search for myself, amid the confusion that followed the revolution. That Christmas Eve when I wandered in the heavy snow. The inn, the cold soup, the cheap rug, the elderly Jewish man who knew something but was hiding something, and… the charred stump of a fir tree. And here I was now, heading towards Savinski!

'But, how did you know about the timid-looking dog? Was that just your imagination, or was it something you heard?'

I had no idea where to begin. I thought Yan's story was true. That fir tree was still alive in a corner of my heart. It was real. And it grew a new branch every year. When I was in a bout of depression, that story about a cat and a fir tree was just a made-up story. Then, after a night, the story crept back quietly to my heart, like the only sunlight which reaches into a dismal city. But her story and the actual stars in my hands threw me into confusion again. That vision of a northern town that Yan had had that day in the meadow at the end of the summer was now here in my hand. Could a story have given rise to a dream and a dream to reality. These stars in my hand were real enough. Or perhaps it was just a series of coincidences?

'No, it's neither. It is a true story.'

And I started telling Lili the story of 'The Christmas in the meadow' that Yan told me.

The train was running through the marshes, going over the occasional little iron bridge. Every time my story was interrupted by the sound of the train going over a bridge, she leant closer. I carried on telling her the story smelling the faint scent of that white rose.

When he first told me the story, I had taken notes, and had read and re-read these so many times, I could remember everything by heart.I told the story as if I was Yan, trying hard to avoid adding anything or changing it in any way. I lost count of the number of stations we passed in that time. A series of station buildings painted pale colours with vast platforms appeared and disappeared... blue and white, pale yellow and cream, pale green.

At one station, she jumped off the train onto the platform – she did actually jump – and bought two apples from an old lady who was selling things on the platform.

I started talking again, biting the apple. She bit into hers, engrossed in my story.

She was clearly moved by what I had to tell. In the end, she put down her half-eaten apple and looked out of the window, with tear-filled eyes, at the silver birch woods and the telegraph poles flying past.

'...I have no need to be forgiven, no need of God's mercy. We have no sins. There is no need for God at all in this meadow where neither past nor future exists. For this meadow is a place for those who know loneliness and sadness. Mercy, jealousy, hatred, and salvation, have no place here...'

When I said this, she was still looking out of the window

with her tear-filled eyes and continued the story herself in a low voice,

'And as this world draws to a close, we find ourselves naked and without shelter. We are the memories of everything to arise from creation since the beginning of time. And that is why we breathe, love, cry and look after each other, recalling the miracle that took place long ago.'

I didn't know how to respond to her beautiful words.
'And, what do you think?'
'Well… I?'
'Do you think you don't need God either, like Yan?'
'Well… I wouldn't deny God as strongly as Yan did, but I think of myself as an atheist.   I mean, I think God may forgive us for denying his existence…'

'Doesn't that mean that you are accepting the existence of God? Is that your atheism?'
She couldn't hold back her laughter and covered her mouth with both hands. I laughed out loud, too.
We were relaxed with each other already. The trunks of the silver birches going past the window seemed to be radiating laughter too.

'Do you mind if I ask your name?' she said.
I suddenly realised that even though she'd introduced

herself, I'd been so engrossed in the silver stars she found that I'd completely forgotten to do the same. But, …

'You don't have to tell me if you don't want to.'

'Well, you see…' I answered sadly, 'the author of this story never gave me a name.'

'Oh,' she said, looking rather downcast. 'I'm sorry. I shouldn't have asked. Perhaps, the author doesn't like humans very much, even though he's very kind to animals.'

'But, humans are a species of animal.'

'That's true, isn't it? Then, perhaps he's just nicer to non-human animals.'

'… Perhaps.'

' But if that's true, I must be portrayed as a nasty character, don't you think?'

'Oh, no, that's not true at all.'

'Do you think so?' she said, looking into my eyes with a cheeky expression.

In fact, what was attractive about her would have been lost in any detailed description. I think the author's judgement was right about that. He was letting things be, without overdoing it.

And as for me, well he seems to have ignored me altogether from the very beginning.

'Oh, we've been sidetracked completely. Please tell me the rest of the story. Quick, quick.'

I started talking again.

'… But, for me there was nothing to pray for. At this very moment, here in this world, all that exists are the lonely Station of Savinski, the buildings surrounding the square, myself, the streetlamps, and the cold misty rain. No, then I've forgotten something. At this very moment, from that same row of poplar trees where the rat has just disappeared, a rook is about to walk into the square, hunched over as usual with all the melancholy of the world on his back…'

At that moment, the train stopped at a strange station. The outside of the station building was magnificent, but the interior was dull and drab.
Suddenly, a speech echoed over the loudspeakers.
'To become an engineer of the human soul… to safeguard against the conventional style of romanticism… which is to say… creating a life which doesn't exist and characters which don't exist… safeguarding against romanticism as a yearning after some form of utopia. Materialistic… Romanticism is not irrelevant to our literature, but is to be replaced by a new form of romanticism … revolutionary Romanticism.'*

*From a speech by Andrei Zhdanov, delivered at the first Soviet Writers' Alliance Conference on 17 August 1934.

The speech ended with a storm of applause.

She looked over her shoulder – something we had all become accustomed to doing, of late – and whispered to me mischeviously,
'Well I'd like to tell Yan's story to that big cheese. Imagine the rat and the rook walking up to him! Yan's story is anti-revolutionary… hang on… no, it's super-Romanticsm.'

After a while, she looked a little sad,
'Yan created a realm of pure imagination, a place beyond the human world, he's probably looking down on us from there now. Or… It may become separated altogether from the human world… We have already been left behind…'
'No, that's not true. Listen and I'll tell you what happened.'

As soon as the train left the station I went on with the story. Half the sky was covered with a bank of cloud that stretched all the way to the eastern horizon. The sunlight had long since left our compartment, but still lit the meadows and woods outside the window. The carriages cast long box-like shadows across the banks of the railway.

After staring at the bright light outside, it was difficult to see her face clearly in the dim light of the compartment. But as my eyes became used to the darkness I could see she was smiling gently.

'The season passed quickly and the only thing left behind was my consciousness. My thoughts went backwards and forwards along the railway between Savinski and the fir tree in the meadow, so often that they began to freeze in the snow.'

When the train pulled into another station and was about to stop, she grabbed my hand excitedly and said, 'Oh Look! Mr Mysterious Romantic! This is Savinski!'

And there, unmistakably was Savinski Station. Nothing had changed after thirteen years. The three silver birches standing diagonally in front had become much more magnificent, but the way they leant against each other was exactly the same. And the window of the café, too. In fact, very little may have changed since Yan's time when he visited here around the turn of the century, thirty-four years ago. This station would always be the same for decades or even hundreds of years from now.

Even if all the people in this town died out, and there was no one new moving in, the station building would go on standing there, weathering slowly.
'Look, there are the old ladies selling eggs and honey! Let's make gogol-mogol like Yan did.'
She asked me excitedly if I had a cup.

I opened my old suitcase and took out an enamel cup and a spoon.

'Wonderful, Mr Romantic!'

She opened the door and jumped out onto the platform.

I opened the window wide and leant out trying to catch the sunlight and the August breeze.

But the light was low in the west and even when I leant out, I was still in the shade of the carriage.

She was standing on the platform, the sunlight lighting her whole body. Holding her hair back from her face because of the breeze. The soft hair on the nape of her neck shone gold when the old lady put some honey into the cup.

'Lili! The train will leave you behind!' I shouted smiling. She waved to me smiling as well. She ran back, holding the cup in her right hand, and stood by the window. We looked at each other in the shade of the carriage. The train gave a jolt and started moving.

'Quick! Quick!' I shouted again.

She held onto the handrail of the steps with a cheeky smile on her face.

When she returned to her seat, she was stirring the

mixture with the spoon quickly, trying to froth it up.
'I got some milk as well,' she said excitedly.

As she smiled, the melancholy of Savinski Station began to disappear behind us.

She really was heading into the future, I thought to myself.
'Anyway, go on with the story!'
I nodded silently.

'When I had finished decorating the tree, I sat down on the grass on one of the few patches of green that were left. I felt tired and content, and I felt that this little tree with its moons and stars didn't really belong to me. It was there for everyone, for the Pike, the Rat and his orphans, the Rook, the old vodka drinker, the women selling eggs and honey, the foxes and the rabbits who like skating, the Gypsy violinist, the lady selling Christmas decorations, the kitten in the café, and the old lady with her potatoes. It was for all of them, and for many more besides. It was there for everyone.'

So you see… we haven't been left behind at all. Yan's realm of imagination is still with us.'

'Really? So we belong to their group of friends as well?'

'Of course we do!'

Then, we reached the last few lines.
I spoke each word slowly and carefully as if they were the final words of a magnificent Nativity Play.

'As twilight fell, the wind grew cold and it was time to leave. As I looked back, the silver star on the top of the tree was glinting in the setting sun, half gold and half silver. It was more beautiful and more sacred than the cross on the spire of a cathedral.

But at the same time, it was still only a symbol.

I jumped onto the train, the Savinski branch-line…

…feeling a secret glow inside.'

There was a beautiful silence between us. A silence that seemed to last forever…

'Would… would you like to try some of this gogol-mogol I've made?'

She held the cup towards me with both hands. I wrapped my hands around hers gently and took the cup. When I looked up she was crying. We were both so moved, I held the cup tight but could hardly drink. A gentle silence came over us again.

She put her hand in her jacket pocket and took out the silver stars. She sat staring out of the window at the landscape that seemed to go on forever. But what was projected on her brown eyes were neither the clouds, nor the forests, nor the little white flowers beside the railway; projected on her eyes were the scenes from this story. The path Yan walked down the hill, the view from the top of the rock, the footprints of the animals left in the snow in the forests, Savinski Station Square, the little alley where the rat lived, the row of poplar trees, the station café, and the fir tree in the meadow. She was dreaming the whole story again.

After a while she said, 'it really doesn't matter to me whether this story was your creation or Yan's.
It's a lovely story, anyway. It doesn't even matter whether it was made-up or if it actually happened.'

'It is true Lili! It's a true story.'
'Yes, but it's difficult to believe a cat talking to a human, to several humans in fact, and for them to talk to him without being the least bit surprised by a talking cat?'

She was smiling, and seemed to be enjoying herself teasing me.

'But then Yan could speak Russian and Polish, and apparently a little bit of Turkish, too.
That I don't understand, but… Cod language… Yan told me that himself. He talked to me, anyway.'
I regretted mentioning the Cod language because she nearly burst into laughter as soon as I said it.

'OK, so it was a story Yan made up, and you heard it from him. I believe you.'
'No, that's not it. It's a true story. It really happened.'
'So, did you really go looking for a fir tree with a silver star on the top of it in a blizzard thirteen years ago?'
'Yes.'
She sighed.
'But if the tree had been burnt, even if you swore that it was a true story, no one will ever know for sure whether it really happened or not, will they?'
'No, but I wonder if that old Jewish man at the inn was telling the truth… I'm still not sure even now.'
'Then, didn't you think of searching for it again?'
'Certainly I did, but the following year, 1922, I went abroad. I wandered around… Berlin, Paris, Istanbul, everywhere. But I've given up on it now because it's been over thirty years since Yan decorated the tree.'

'Really? Everything sinks back into the past, doesn't it?' she said. 'Everything. Even we are already illusions of our past talking to each other for the benefit of the readers.'

'But even if that's true I don't mind, particularly. I always seem to end up as a mixture of the author's past memories and reminiscences, like a badly made omelette. There is only past and no future when you look around you.'

'Well not quite. I mean you believe Yan's story is the truth, don't you?
And you live on in future memories.'
'And what about you? Do you believe in Yan's story, now?'
'Yes,' she answered.

But I could tell she still didn't.

The mist began to settle on the silver birch woods. The white paint on the lower half of the telegraph poles flickered past in an endless stream. And in front of it, was her face, looking slightly sad.

'Eventually, all our happy memories will be sealed in glass marbles, and every time you remember them they will be put into a glass jar with a wide rim. And nobody will remember where all those jars are kept. But, lonely and unhappy memories are like tiny pebbles on a clear riverbed. Sometimes, in the fast flow of consciousness they will be brought up to the surface, at other times they will sink deep into the subconscious, and will be carried down to the river mouth of life so slowly that they won't seem to move at all. So the only memories you remember before you die, are the sad ones. But is there anything more beautiful than those lonely, sad memories which have been polished again and again?'

All the stations we were going through were hidden in the fog. Only the sound of the train going over the points, and the dim lights of the signals indicated that we were approaching a station, and the screech of the brakes made their existence a reality. My eyes were peering out into that world of fog while listening to Lili talking.

'There is a poem, I wonder if you've heard of it?'
'How does it go?' I answered smiling.

'Winter Celebration

The future is not enough
Old things and New things are not enough
In the middle of the room, eternity
becomes a sacred fir tree ...'

'Say it with me.

The future is not enough
Old things and New things are not enough
In the middle of the room, eternity
becomes a sacred fir tree'

'Why don't we replace a word in this poem? Like this,

The future is not enough
Old things and New things are not enough
In the middle of a meadow, eternity
becomes a sacred fir tree'

'In the middle of a meadow, eternity becomes a sacred fir tree... Strange, it's as if Yan's story became a poem. Yan decorated that young fir tree and it became eternal...'
'Exactly.'
'Does this story - Yan's story have a title?'
'A title? I've never thought about it before. It's not really a story or a novel. It's a true story.'
'But, if sometime in the future, you write a book about this story... I'm being serious... please call it 'The Celebration in the Meadow"
'Of course, I will... And thank you,' I said with an awkward smile.

It was some time after nine o'clock in the evening, but the sun had still not gone down. There was a slight fog and the brightness of the sky was fading.

'We won't even be able to recognise the deserted station if it stays like this,' she said looking outside. I had just been thinking the same thing.

'Well, no, not in this fog.'
I was remembering a part of the poem Yan wrote watching the fog going by.

'Going home on a train thorough the fog
My stars, go on shining
Even when they fall to the ground,
They go on shining
Even when they're lost,
They go on shining
In the memory we all share,
Forever.'

She had fallen asleep, overcome by the fatigue of the long journey. The silver stars were also sleeping in her hand. Outside, evening did not fall until the lights in the carriage were dimly lit. She was still fast asleep. I was feeling sleepy too, but kept rubbing my eyes and staring at the world where nothing except fog was visible. I no longer had any idea whether or not we had past the deserted station.

I drifted into a shallow, restless sleep. Kept awake by my desire not to miss…

When I heard the wheel going over the points I was suddenly wide awake. I looked out of the window, the dense fog was thinning, and suddenly, black conifer forests appeared here and there in the transparent air as if the curtains had been drawn apart. Then the forest came to an end and there was a meadow sloping upward towards the darkening sky.

On the top of it, was a single fir tree, with a star shining at the top of it.

I saw it for only a brief moment.

Before the forest hid everything from view again.

'I saw it! I saw Yan's star! I really saw it!'
'What? Where?'
She suddenly opened her eyes and even though she was still half-asleep she began desperately wiping away the condensation to look out of the window.

'Perhaps it was just the evening star or some other bright star over a fir tree.'

And she was dragged off by the sleep-fairy she could not resist.

I stared at Lili's face, with tears in my eyes.

And even when a tear fell onto her auburn hair and trickled down the side of her gentle sleeping face, she still showed no sign of waking.

The Savinski branch-line had been closed for some time. Summer weeds grew between the tracks, and birds wandered on the banks looking for insects and small berries. The deserted station weathered quietly and slowly, with only the song of the birds for company.

The station building was left as it was and the station café didn't change at all except that it just catered for customers coming in from the town.

The gypsies disappeared and there was no-one left to play music in the café. Instead, a Jewish violinist who had survived the Purges came to play old waltzes and tangos which were popular a long time ago, in order to earn a crust. Later on, he just came when he felt like it.

The kitten that used to peep into the café window ended up being adopted by the old man who liked vodka. It had four kittens, and when they grew up, each of them had four more, and each of those… So there was soon a whole line of kittens sitting on the window-ledge peeping into the café. The old ladies who sold things at the station had long been replaced by a new generation of old ladies. The current ones looked exactly the same and did their business at the bus station for the long distance buses which stopped here on their way to the far north.

The battered old bus waited with its engine rattling, and departed somehow over a road of rocks and potholes.

In 1920 the anti-revolutionary group was defeated and General Miller escaped on an iceboat. And the grey-haired Captain of the iceboat was none other than the blond sailor who Yan had met on the train.

The town of Savinski itself had scarcely changed. Although no-one came out of the station anymore and stood looking at the square. The buildings surrounding it were still standing, though the architecture was the style of a bygone era. The theatre closed down although whether this was because it was suppressed by the new ideology, or simply because customers stopped coming, is hard to say.

The row of poplar trees grew old and tired, and once summer was over they shed their yellow leaves and fell asleep.

The short story writer passed away two or three years after Yan decorated the fir tree, in a resort in Southern Germany.

The crane said farewell to the writer about a year before that and flew off somewhere or other.

The Rat and the Rook are still alive and well. As Yan said, they are a part of eternity.

And as for the question most readers are probably wondering: what happened to Lili and Mr Romantic? Well I think we've watched over them enough. I think we should just leave them be.

Finally, as for the fir tree with the silver star on the top, that's something you'll have to go and search for yourselves. Even if you don't manage to find it, it would still be a journey you will never forget.

Chekhov and his crane

A letter from Chekhov

'I checked out of a health resort in Nice just to make this film… and all you can see in it are my glasses and walking stick…

What's more, I was treated like a nuisance and eventually ignored altogether by a very stubborn cat. I shall begin with the conclusion… this work is thoroughly self-indulgent and individualistic. Purely. …and purity is the only word I can use to praise this work at the present time.

The shooting of the film is going well. The producer has been rushing about all the time trying to raise the money and on the rare occasions he comes out to the location, he shouts at people to hurry up and finish quickly. The director is apparently 'avant-garde' and famous for his 'technique-orientated' work. This is his own particular pet-phrase but no-one around him knows what he means by this. In one scene, he spent a whole day instructing The Pike and had to be carried down to the river on a stretcher because he has weak lungs. The rook was told to stand vacantly under a tree, but he was forgotten about after the shooting and was found unconscious under the same tree a week later. All is going well. It is almost frightening. The main character, the cat, keeps pulling out the crane's feathers whenever he gets a chance and playing Cowboys and Indians with the rat. The rat always wants to command the cavalry.

Listen to me. I must be suffering from some kind of mental illness. Last night I had a dream that all the animals in the cast came floating down from the sky and acted their scenes perfectly. They live somewhere beyond our imagination. I wonder if you understand me. There are still worlds we don't understand in this universe of ours. Well, the scene with myself and the crane is about to start again. Don't forget: they came from the sky.'

Extracts from an Interview with the Director

Q: First of all, which genre does this work fit into? A novel, a prose-poem, or a film/animation script?
- I don't like the word animation because animations in this country are very poor. So, if you wish to categorise it in terms of visual art, it's a film. In terms of words, it is a poetic story.

Q: I think there are some animated films such as those by Norshtein in Russia and Karel Zeman in Czechoslovakia which are deeper than many non-animated films. Would you agree?

- True. Strangely there seemed to be room for masterpieces like these under communism, but it is difficult to find backers for such projects now. Under capitalism profit is more important than beauty.

Q: By the way, I hear this story was originally inspired by a picture.
- How do you know that? Who told you? Yes, it was the picture of a cat decorating a fir tree in the middle of a meadow (page 166). It was sold in a café called the Odessa-Istanbul café. Have you heard of it? A very well-known café, legendary in fact, Od…

Q: As a Christmas card?

- That's how I thought of it in the first place, but then the image came to mind and I wanted to start drawing it, as is always the case with me. Initially, I imagined a picture of Yan standing on a ladder decorating one of several conifer trees, but I realised it was too much trouble drawing so many trees. Also, because I liked meadows anyway, I drew a single tree and it looked very sad. It's my favourite picture to this day. It's not actually a story about Christmas at all.

Q: What do you intend to express in this story?

- That's a rather banal question – It would be difficult to answer that fully. Basically, I just wanted to create an entirely different world to our dull human one.

Q: Why aren't there many human characters appearing in your works?

- There are more than enough works on humans already. That leaves only two possibilities: either you kill off all the human characters, or you don't draw them in the first place. I chose the latter, i.e. I want to start from scratch to create a world where there are no humans. Also, humans are difficult to draw because they have no hair. They are strange, and not particularly cute because all their skin is exposed.

Q: Is there any significance in the years, 1921, 1900-2, 1934?

- That is a good question. It is beyond us to imagine what must have happened in that thirty years not only in politics but also in the world of art and culture. I decided to use 1934 to allow me to bring in Zhdanov's speech. It was that speech which outlined the communist idea of ultra-realism. It has to be said, though, there is *some* merit in ultra-realism. Keilov was assassinated towards the end of that year and the Stalin's reign of terror was at its peak.

Q: How did the shooting of the scenes go?

- I'm not very satisfied. I want to re-do it if there is time. The pictures are too purely descriptive. I normally prefer viewpoints which depart from the main theme. There is depth in a moment which has no meaning other than a mental pause.

Q: Your last work was also set in and around Russia, can you not write a work based in Japan?

- I find it difficult in such a confined space. Are you suggesting I write about some urban landscape where a cat, a fox, and a racoon squabble with each other? There are lots of high-rise blocks of apartments, and they coincidentally meet round the corner. In other words, such a country doesn't appeal to me.

Q: But aren't you cheating by shooting something in a place the audience doesn't know?

- I find that a most impertinent suggestion. Well, for a start, most of the audience will not be experts on the Russian landscape and in any case, despite what people say I have neither the money nor the influence. Anything that's not set in France, Italy, or America isn't popular anyway.

Q: So there aren't many people who come to see your work, you mean?

(The Director was muttering something to himself at this time.)

Q: There is one scene I don't understand. It must have been in the fifth journey where Yan went back to Savinski. Why is he not wearing boots? I'm sure the felt boots were…

- That's not important. They were wet, inside and out. Look, he's got dirty feet. He's drying them in the waiting room or somewhere. And his gloves as well.

Q: I'm impressed that Chekhov appeared.

- Well, because it's my work. It's a once in a lifetime opportunity, isn't it? For him, I mean.

Q: As for the music, why did that violinist disappear after

singing the aria from Matthew?

- Yan doesn't like the self-important religious world. Also, being animals they are free from sin and so have no need of mercy. I don't particularly like Bach either.

Q: You really are very strange. By the way, that scene of the gigantic rat, were you being sarcastic towards Russian avant-garde artists like Malevich or Filonov?

- Not at all. But, when you're at my age, you're moved by the pictures of Isaac Levitan.

Q: Well, what's next?

- There is a bird called the Hawfinch which is a bit cheeky but very sweet. This bird … (Here we ran out of time, but he carried on talking to himself. We left quietly so that he didn't notice us going.)

the Rook (still waiting)

the End

A note on the author

Author and illustrator Jun Machida was born in Tokyo in 1951.

For many years he ran the Odessa-Istanbul Café in Shibuya, where his charming pictures of Yan the cat were first exhibited. These attracted such attention from his customers that he began writing *The Private Papers of Yan*.

And so was born the first in a series of stories: *Yan and the Pike*.

yan and the pike

written and illustrated by

Jun Machida

Yan is a cat.
A cat who does things carefully. Things like making tea, or
mushroom soup, or polishing the hinges of his door.
One day, while he is dozing peacefully, there is a knock at
the door. He opens it. And there before him, stands a
solitary pike.
'Hello. My name is Pike.'
And so it was, the two became friends.

yan and the pike is the first book in the Yan series.

ISBN   0-9534205-4-X
Price: £ 7.99

yan and the pike's violin

written and illustrated by

Jun Machida

yan and the pike's violin continues the story of Yan the cat, and sees him re-united with his old friend Mr Pike.

Since we last met him, Mr Pike has taken up playing the violin. Something he does with great enthusiasm. The gentle, and taciturn Mr Cod also makes an appearance.

Charming and surreal by turns, the stories of Yan the cat are already bestsellers in China, Japan, and Korea. Now, for the first time his adventures are being told in English.

ISBN   0-9544959-4-2
Price: £ 7.99

All titles are available direct from

acorn book company
PO Box 191, Tadworth
Surrey KT20 5YQ

POST FREE IN THE UK

Cheques payable to acorn book company.
or email your order to sales@acornbook.co.uk

acorn book company

is an independent
publisher of small, high quality editions.

We also operate a mail order website.

For more information
please visit us at:
www.acornbook.co.uk